The **FIRE**

ONSLAUGHT

A Sci-Fi Action Novel

Nathaniel A Rose

This book is a work of fiction. Names, characters, places and incidents are products of the authors' imagination or are used fictitiously. Any resemblance to actual events or locales or persons, living or dead, is entirely coincidental.

ISBN: 978-0-9855818-5-5

First Edition: March 2014

An *Original* Publication by Brothers-In-Arms Publishing

Cover Art & Written By: Nathaniel A Rose

Edited By: Ingrun Mann

<u>Special Thanks</u>

My parents for their support
My friends for their encouragement
My brother Dan for his insight
Eden Spring for her inspiration

Chapter One: Trials & Tribulations

January 1st, 2142

During the early morning hours Lieutenant General May appointed Captain Dyson the head of security. He was to oversee the registration of all personnel inside the airport terminal. Soldiers—both regular and NARC—stood in long lines for identification. For the most part, NARC took control of all combat operations and integrated remnant US military assets into their command structure.

Without a proper chain of command and not enough officers to form even a small squad, First Lieutenant Hawk found himself the commanding officer of the remaining 82nd units. He and his company were given orders right after checking in with NARC security, and found themselves mounting up for patrols that very afternoon.

To a combat veteran like Hawk, this wasn't unlike the occupation of a foreign country. You couldn't leave the base perimeter without orders or being armed. The conflict in North Korea a year ago had played out in much the same way, and in Hawk's mind, Detroit was no different. The only exceptions were the following: one, aliens were the enemy now, and two, the fight was taking place at home.

This time around the Rules of Engagement (ROE) were simple: engage any hostile, non-human intelligence, and suppress threats to the security and survival of the human race. Interpretation of the ROEs was left to the discretion of the individual field commanders.

As night was about to fall, Lieutenant Hawk led his squad from the airport into the heart of downtown Detroit. The group included his wife Angel, who had been issued a female version of the Firehawk Battle Suit which her husband gave her from the stash he kept secret. She also wore the FAITH-33, or Female Artificial Intelligence Tactical Helmet, which provided the same functionality as her husband's protective head gear, but allowed her to put her hair in a ponytail and let it hang out the back. In addition, Angel carried the M19A2 pistol and its holster on her right thigh as well as a 5.56mm version of the M71 Light Assault Rifle.

The M71 was much more compact than the standard M22A3 version, but didn't pack as much punch. However, it featured a built-in laser aiming device, ammo counter, and range finder, and was primarily used by medics, support, and civilian personnel. On the battlefield, it wasn't quite as good as the M22A3 as far as range and damage were concerned. On the other hand, its size categorized it as a sub-machine gun that was deemed ideal for urban warfare.

Most females in the US military carried this light assault weapon. Angel had volunteered her services as a combat medic to her husband's team. Her background as a nurse and bachelor's degree in medicine made her an incredibly invaluable asset to his squad, and as such Captain Dyson had granted her a field commission to the grade of second lieutenant.

Shane's younger brother Marshal had worked as an engineer before the Cataclysm, and he was re-issued equipment after he registered with security. Lieutenant Hawk had put in a request to General May that his brother be placed on his team. The general had authorized his petition as a personal favor. Marshal received a Magnum Battle Suit, which was effectively a walking tank. This heavy body armor with a built-in exoskeleton made up the MXS-233. The exoskeleton provided ordinary humans with incredible armor protection as well as enhanced robotic strength and speed. MXS wearers were capable of lifting great weights, could leap over gaping holes, and wield heavy equipment with relative ease.

The face plate consisted of tinted, transparent aluminum which obscured the wearer's features and represented the standard of all NARC and US military issued helmets. Large shoulder shields guaranteed additional protection for the base of the neck and collar bone, while the chest plate reinforced the wearer's torso. Forearms and legs were encased in thick armor with special, built-in capabilities.

But what really set the Magnum apart from all other Battle Suits in the NARC and US military inventory was the MARG-3 Cannon. Five inches across in bore diameter, the weapon was eight feet long with a jet booster recoil reduction system that activated automatically when fired. This devastating weapon launched a highly sophisticated, five pound, composite "Glasser" round at Mach three, creating an ear shattering sonic boom when fired.

The Glasser—capable of a number of combat applications—featured a mini, electromagnetic rail system imbedded in the gun's inner core. This rail system pulled the round forward with a highly advanced mechanism that enabled the projectile to strike targets up to five miles downrange. The "glass" portion of the round (the outer casing and actually a super dense, semi-transparent glass/plastic alloy) Maynsed in such a way that it drove the inner core (sabot) into thick armor with exponential force. Also, after leaving the barrel, the Glasser round could be set to detonate anywhere past twenty-five yards. This pivotal feature allowed the round to penetrate a wall and ignite, shattering the room on the other side with utmost precision.

Although Marshal Hawk was happy about the Magnum Suit and MARG-3 Cannon, he grumbled when he only received the rank of a lowly NARC private. After all, he held a degree. Meanwhile, Harris—Shane's older brother—completed some basic refresher training with other NARC volunteer soldiers. Afterwards he was re-assigned to Shane's squad at the latter's request.

In the last couple of days the older Private Hawk had proven himself an excellent shot and was issued the Lone Wolf Battle Suit and SR-25 Laser Sniper Rifle. His experience might have been limited as far as snipers went, but he was much more experienced than Marshal. Harris had served in the U.S. Marine Corps twelve years ago. And although the three-day crash course in military etiquette and tactics left him tired and exhausted, Harris was ready for action.

Sergeant Almazan had also joined them and was carrying his favorite rifle, the M450C Squad Automatic Weapon. The M450C only fired in bursts and packed a hell of a punch. When firing three to four rounds, the rifle was unsurpassed in accuracy, especially in comparison with its predecessors. The rounds were larger than the M22A3 types and featured a drum mounted under the breech. The drum first fed rounds into the chamber by means of a belt and then onto electromagnetic rails bored into the barrel. This was a common feature for all US military weapons, which launched projectiles downrange at near Mach two blazing speeds and could tear up almost any armored structure.

The sonic boom associated with the Magnums' MARG-3 Cannon didn't apply to this particular weapon. Although the MARG-3 packed the massive Glasser round, it didn't feature the rails that bore into the barrels of these state-of-the-art rifles. Bullets from American weapons accelerated after they were launched from the barrel, unlike the MARG-3 which did so from the bolt.

While the men prepared for more rounds of battle, Amanda helped June watch the children. In between breaks she often sat down to read a book on ancient myths as well as another one she had found on vampires, werewolves, and monsters. With the world growing ever more chaotic by the day and aliens invading Earth, Almazan's wife had become fascinated by the mystery of such creatures and wanted to read up on anything she could find about these mythical beasts of yore.

Lieutenant Shane Hawk was a natural leader. Always the consummate professional on duty, he now had to let go of some of the formalities as his new squad was made up of a ragtag group of his closest friends and family. Still, Shane maintained his professionalism around his peers while relaxing out in the field. He carried the M71A2 assault rifle—his weapon of choice—together with the M19A2 pistol. After the encounter with "Karna," he always wore the Firehawk Battle Suit, and carried with him a satchel of incendiary grenades.

Ready for action, he had every squad member's position tag on his Heads-Up-Display along with a mini-map of the area of town they were about to patrol. Small robotic drones the size and shape of baseballs hovered hundreds of feet above to give them pinpoint locations of every soldier in the city like a low altitude GPS satellite system. Information could be instantly transmitted to the drones and back down to anyone wearing a NARC tactical helmet, Battle Suit, robot, jet, or ATH-33.

General May had assigned Detroit's southern end to the forty-nine 82nd survivors. It consisted of buildings and small homes that only covered a thirty square mile area, while the more numerous NARC Battalions took over larger sections of the city. Captain Dyson was the Officer-In-Charge of Operations, and Lieutenant Hawk was to report to him after each completed patrol with his Special Forces squad.

On the first day of the New Year all contact with the outside world had suddenly been cut off. The Cheyenne Mountain Complex—the temporary home of the President of the United States and NORAD—was completely destroyed, and there were no survivors. That report was the last to come out of the western United States.

For the first time since time immemorial, there were no New Year's celebrations as NARC and 82nd patrols worked eighteen hour shifts rescuing survivors, helping a few thousand people find food and shelter for the night, and fighting off alien creatures. Some subdued commemorations took place among civilians, who mostly hugged and said a few softly spoken prayers.

Meanwhile, Lieutenant Hawk and his squad hunkered down in an abandoned café, waiting for a freak storm caused by residual energy to pass. They waited patiently as thousands of basketball-sized teardrops of ice fell from the sky, shattering or severely damaging everything they hit.

The freak storm already had them pausing for an hour, leaving everyone bored with nothing to do. Lieutenant Hawk lit up a cigarette, a habit picked up in the last couple of days due to the stress of managing his men and teams. He preferred any menthol brand, but wasn't particular when his pack ran out, forcing him to "bum" one off someone else. Angel had also taken up the habit, while refusing to smoke around the kids. At first Shane didn't care who saw him, but after his wife lectured him on smoking around minors, he stopped as well.

Frustrated by the wait, Hawk took a drag, inhaled, and let it out with a long sigh. Angel was sitting in a chair across from him as he looked out a broken window, passing the cigarette between his fingers to hers. Meanwhile, Harris, Marshal, and Almazan were playing a game of cards. They chatted quietly amongst themselves, but had Angel noticed her husband's groan and sidled up next to him. He was leaning against the backside of a booth and gave her a long look.

"What's the matter punkin?" she asked softly and with a bit of concern. He stared at the broken tiles and shattered glass on the dirty floor.

"Ah...," he mumbled, "Nothing really."

But she knew something was bothering him, "Are you OK?"

"Yeah, I'm fine, I'm just trying to think of a place that's safe to move the kids into with us outside of that dank airport," he told her, still staring at the floor.

"I heard some of the NARC troops have already started finding shelters near the airport," she told him. He shrugged; he didn't much care for living that close to their base of operations as it was always busy. However, it was probably the safest area in the whole city. On the other hand, it was more prone to attack as well.

The sound of breaking snow crystals on the streets outside started to lessen, while the size of the "tears of ice" diminished too as the storm moved east over the Detroit River. Lieutenant Hawk put his helmet on and Angel did the same, knowing that they were about to leave. A few minutes later Shane stepped outside with his weapon at the ready and scanned the neighborhood for any signs of danger. Angel told the men still playing cards, "Hey guys, let's get going," picked up her M71 rifle, and left the café.

Immediately, Almazan gathered the cards off the table and stuffed them in his cargo pocket. Harris and Marshal donned their helmets, grabbed their weapons, and hurried outside with the sergeant who was carrying his M450C by the handle. Hawk commanded, "All right, let's check out the church down there. Let's go see if anyone is home. Churches are symbols of refuge and hope for people, so let's see what we can find."

Immediately, his fearless brother Marshal decided to do a little recon as the team followed. "But if I catch on fire from going inside, you're putting me out!" he pointed at his older sibling with a laugh in his voice.

"Hey, I don't go to church either dude. Who's gonna put me out if I spontaneously combust?" Harris chuckled.

"Don't worry guys, I got you!" Almazan squeezed between them and put his hands on their shoulders.

"Great that makes me feel so much better," Marshal tried to be serious.

"Hey now," Almazan grinned, "I'm not *that* bad." But Marshal just shook his head, while Harris rolled his eyes.

"Come on guys, let's get moving," Shane urged impatiently. Everyone nodded and they began walking down the street in a wedge formation with the heaviest firepower—Marshal in his Magnum Battle Suit—in the back. They could see that the church spire was broken at the top, the result of continued acts of lootings and vandalism during the past week. Approaching the house of worship, they also noticed an awful smell emanating from the building. Each of their environmental suits automatically kicked in the oxygen supply and gas filters to limit the noxious fumes. It wasn't the best equipment in the world and certainly had its weaknesses, but it helped. Still, amid the familiar odor of ash and dust, the squad unmistakably recognized the stench of rotting flesh.

With a heavy heart, Lieutenant Hawk hastened up the walkway and a flight of steps to the church's double front doors. The entrance sported the broken remnants of stained glass windows, and one depicted the face of the Virgin Mary in the most frightful fashion. The majority of the colorful window had shattered and only half of her somewhat melted face remained.

Slightly spooked, Shane tried to open the doors, but found them locked. Backing up a bit, he kicked the entrance between the handles. The doors swung open as the glass windows disintegrated completely. A ghastly, greenish-gray cloud slithered along the floor to the outside. For a moment, the eerie fog enveloped everything, making it difficult for Shane to get a good look at the building's interior.

As the gas subsided, Hawk's squad carefully entered the foyer and noticed hundreds of people on crowded benches. Most were sitting upright, some with their heads tilted back and eyes wide open, their lower jaws gaping. Others were kneeling in the pews, locked in praying positions. All were dead. Their flesh had turned grey; their hair was ragged and frayed. It was a horrific sight as the casualties included men, women, and children of all ages.

Alarmed, Lieutenant Hawk turned on the built-in flashlight at the front of his weapon. Every gruesome detail was visible now, since the rotting flesh exposed people's innermost secrets. One man had a bionic eye, another a cybernetic leg, while a third revealed a cybernetic arm, which had been illegal without a medical license. The putrefying corpses looked diseased and exhibited wounds ravaged by either a virus or chemical agent.

"What happened to these people?" Harris was revolted. Angel nearly threw up in her helmet, but managed to hold back at the last minute. They made their way to the altar, and Hawk spotted a corpse hunched up against it. The man was dressed in a priest's white robe and wore a bishop's miter. He still held a long staff in his right arm, while the other rested on the altar next to a cylinder of Nanmetic Gas.

Before the Cataclysm, this particular gas had been primarily used for eradicating insect infestations in third world countries. Even a small amount could do serious harm to humans, and it had been outlawed in the United States years ago. Shane suspected that the container on the altar—which was the size of a milk jug—had been sufficient to kill every living thing in the church.

"It looks like they committed mass suicide," Angel spoke over the radio in her helmet. "There are no signs of struggle, no signs of anyone trying to break free. They all went willingly," she swallowed. Shane shook his head in disbelief and read the label on the cylinder. He set it back down, gazing up at the porcelain statue of Christ on the cross that was mounted on the wall behind the altar.

Marshal suddenly spoke up, "Check this out." All heads followed his flashlight beam near the priest's backroom entrance. There on the wall, written in blood, was a message to all that would enter. It read:

GONE TO MEET THE LORD

Shane remembered his studies back in high school, "During the crusades, many people believed that suicide was the path to hell and the priest would cut the suicide's head off, so they would wander around hell eternally deaf, dumb, and blind."

"Wow, that's messed up," Almazan said to himself.

"Should I start lobbing off heads?" Marshal put his hand on the dead priest's shoulder.

Marshal's remark made Shane chuckle, "Nah." He was amused by his brother's crazy idea, "Just leave them be. Let them rest in peace."

"PEACE!?" a gruff man's voice yelled out from behind them. "PEACE!? You think these people died in peace?!" The squad turned around and saw an old man standing in the main doorway. Startled, they instantly aimed their weapons at him. He held a cane in one hand and wore an overcoat, ragged jeans, and work boots. His t-shirt was torn, his white hair balding on his head, but he had a thick, white beard.

Lieutenant Hawk returned to the front of the church with the others in tow. "This is the end of the world young man!" the old man continued to shout. When he opened his mouth, he revealed rows of either missing or rotting teeth with black spots all over his raw gums.

"Yeah, we got that," Marshal interjected coldly. The old man clammed up and shot Marshal a spiteful glance.

"There is no peace left on this planet, hell has come, and we will all suffer the destiny that death will provide us," he harped.

"Life is worth fighting for, you old geezer, and if this truly was the end then none of us would have survived the initial cataclysm," Angel barked, thinking of her kids, and irritated by the old man's arrogance.

"This is the end for us all young lady! Are you so naive in your youth that you fail to realize that which is upon us?!" he pointed at her with an arthritic finger.

Shane now spoke up, "Death is the quick and easy way out mister, we must continue to survive...." He was cut short as the man turned and walked away.

Shane and the others trailed him, but were stopped just outside the doors. A crowd of men and women of all ages had gathered on the lawn as the old man planted himself in the middle of their horseshoe formation. "No one should be afraid of death," he announced dramatically and pulled a pistol from his overcoat, pointing it at a young man's head. He was maybe eighteen and didn't move. In fact, he smiled meekly as death cast its murky shadow upon him.

"I am not afraid to die!" the young man shouted defiantly. Seconds later, the old man pulled the trigger and scattered his victim's brains all over the crowd of doomsayers. Shane, Angel, Almazan, Harris, and Marshal raised their weapons, aiming their sights at the madman.

"I welcome death!" he growled fiercely.

Then his followers stepped in front of him.

"Shoot me…," one young woman pleaded.

"No, take me…," another beckoned.

"Take me…," another man begged. Shane and the others hesitated, unwilling to open fire on these brainwashed people.

"You see?!" the old man barked triumphantly, "We're all ready to die! And you'll join us before the end!" He pointed his pistol at Shane and pulled the trigger. The round rocketed out of the barrel and struck him squarely in the chest plate. Shane merely flinched, because the projectile hadn't been strong enough to puncture his armor. The old man's weapon was only a classic Desert Eagle

.45 caliber pistol. If the barrel had been bored with electromagnetic rails, it might have punctured his armored vest.

Boiling over with rage, Angel aimed her rifle at the old man and fired a single shot. But Shane's attacker was apparently not as eager to die as he claimed. He quickly grabbed a young woman and threw her in Shane's path. The woman didn't struggle as her shoulder exploded into fragments and she fell over dead. In the meantime, the demagogue had slid into the back of the crowd which started surging towards the Special Ops squad.

They were almost zombie-like as they ambled towards them. Their eyes didn't blink, and even the ghastly stench still escaping the church had no effect on the maniacal group. "Kill us," one murmured.

"Yes kill us," another repeated robotically. Then the spooky group began to chant those horrific words.

"Stay back!" Shane yelled. "We don't want to hurt any of you!"

"Don't you fools see that the old coot is only using you?!" Angel hollered at the crowd.

"What are we gonna do Lieutenant?" Almazan nervously backed up.

As the throng began stomping up the first few steps, Shane and his squad found themselves on the defensive. Quickly shutting the church entrance as the fanatics closed in on them, Harris slid a long candle holder between the door handles. "That should hold for a while," he told Shane.

"There's got to be another way out of here," Angel looked around and spotted the door to the sacristy. "Over there, there's one," she pointed towards the back. Almazan immediately ran past the pews and opened it. A hallway to the right led him into an office. Although the windows were boarded up, the room was still well-organized and neat. Unfortunately, there would be no escape without blasting holes into the window boards, Almazan realized, and so he turned around, hurrying down the short corridor.

Meanwhile, Marshal and Shane braced themselves against the entrance as the crowd outside began to bang and rattle. Angel and Harris held their weapons at the ready in case they broke through the doors. The pounding and shoving soon worsened as the entire, hyped-up mob pushed with all their might. Shane and Marshal pressed from the other side, hopeful that the sturdy doors would remain in their frames.

In the back, Almazan had come across another small room, but again there was no way out. It was the priest's vestry, and there was another robe hanging on a rod as well as a shelf with candles mounted on the wall. Almazan began to cheer when he discovered a large, curtained window, but his relief soon evaporated. Upon whipping the curtains open, he looked into the twisted faces of several people staring at him from the outside. One of them bent over and picked up a rock, while another bounced a bottle filled with an unknown liquid and a rag hanging out the top. Part of the rag was already on fire and the man with the rock threw both through the window. Glass shards showered Almazan, but didn't cut through his heavy armor. He jumped back into the hallway as the second man flung another makeshift bomb at him.

The projectiles exploded as the liquids inside caught fire. The priest's robe went up in flames along with the carpet and curtains. Spreading quickly, the blaze snaked up the wall. Some of the fiery fluid had splashed onto Almazan's right leg, and he struggled to extinguish it with his hands.

By this time, Angel had noticed Almazan hurrying towards them. "Did you find a way out?" she lowered her weapon slightly.

"Uh, not unless you'd like a little cocktail," he frowned half-jokingly.

"What are you talking about?" Angel was perplexed. Almazan pointed over his shoulder at the wall. Grey smoke billowed from behind it and was starting to fill the church. Angel's eyes widened with horror as she saw flames licking the altar.

"Shane, we need to get out of here!" she yelled as Almazan leaned against a pew, trying to catch his breath.

"I know Angel!" Shane screamed back without turning around, since the horde on the outside was banging on the doors ever more violently.

"No! Look!" she pointed to the vestry.

Shane finally peered over his shoulder at the burning wall. Then, one of the large, stained glass windows shattered as something landed amidst the benches towards the back of the church. The object burst, resulting in a blistering splash that set pews and corpses on fire. At the same time, the blaze in the back room had finally eaten through the wall and kindled the porcelain statue of Christ. The building's whole rear section stood in flames by now, causing the paint on the porcelain to turn black and melt. It looked as if the whole body of Christ was bleeding black, oily blood.

Terrified, Angel became increasingly impatient, "Get away from the doors!" she screamed at her husband and brother-in-law. When she aimed her rifle at the entrance, both jumped out of the way. Angel opened fire and the rounds blew giant, gaping holes through the entryway. Outside, the squad could hear cries of pain as bullets tore through bodies. The pounding on the doors soon weakened, prompting Marshal to get on his feet. He yanked a heavy candleholder from a table, swung the doors open, and growled at the wounded people on the steps. Others had collapsed in the yard and were now writhing in the grass.

The unhurt fanatics glared at him with unconcealed hatred, but Marshal readied his cannon and charged towards the demented crowd. One man lunged himself at him, but Marshal swung his fist across the individual's mid-section. The sheer strength of the Battle Suit literally severed the man's torso from his lower body and both halves flopped to the ground, spewing guts and blood all over the snow.

Shane and Harris rushed out the doors as two other stained glass windows disintegrated and the benches exploded into fireballs. Angel and Almazan followed the brothers, who indiscriminately launched rounds into the freaks rushing towards them.

Marshal split a man's head in half with an axe-hand strike after being hit by a heavy rock that the attacker had thrown at him. After a few minutes had elapsed, there were maybe a dozen people left standing in the yard. Shane and Harris covered both sides and neutralized assailant after assailant. Angel aimed her M71 rifle at a person sneaking up behind Marshal. Squeezing the trigger, she blew a gaping hole into the man's back and abdomen, which led to more spilt intestines on the ash-covered snow.

Almazan was aiming his M450C machine gun from the hip and let loose a burst into a group of people with knives and crowbars. The rounds from his weapon blew off pieces of flesh and bone and reduced one poor soul's head to a pink, meaty mist. The projectiles also tore up the yard, kicking up ash and snow which formed small dirt clouds.

In as little as ten seconds, the crowd received what they had asked for. After most had been cut down and killed, Shane and his squad raced up the street to seek shelter in the abandoned café once again. Almazan crashed onto a bench, while Marshal and Harris leaned over to catch their breaths.

Angel patted her aching rib cage and massaged a cramp in her side. Shane didn't show any signs of fatigue other than his quickened breathing. Along with the others, he took off his helmet. After braving fire and a crazed mob, everyone was sweating profusely.

Shane let out a long sigh and finally spoke, "Did anyone get that old man?" Angel admitted that she had not, and the others shook their heads as well. Apparently, he had disappeared once the fighting began. Shane frowned. He knew that he would run into this dangerous madman again someday. The brainwashing he had carried out on those poor people at the church would be repeated on others. He would have to be stopped before more innocent individuals fell victim to his murderous designs.

Up the road, the old geezer had retreated to a house a block away from the church. Inside, on the countertop of a kitchen, was a lab of beakers and make-shift pots that contained mixed chemicals and hazardous oxidizers. Several foot-long lead pipes lay around as well, each packed with enough nitro-glycerin to sever the treads on a tank. "These will teach them to embrace death!" he sung merrily as he bounced a pipe in his sweaty, old hand.

In the meantime, Lieutenant Hawk and his squad were waiting for nightfall in the abandoned, freezing café. Almazan had passed out in his chair, while Shane kept a lookout, gazing up and down both ends of the street. "Anything going on out there?" Angel whispered to her husband.

"Nah, nothing. Not a soul, not a sound."

"When are we going to leave?" she asked.

Harris and Marshal were resting in separate booths. Harris was re-tying his long, black ponytail - a token to his best friend John - with a cigarette in his mouth; his brother had dozed off on the table next to him. One hand rested above his head next to the pistol grip of the MARG-3 Cannon, while the other arm was stretched across the top of the booth.

Angel sighed and walked over to another window. She had placed her helmet next to Shane's on a counter. "Shoulda killed that old fart," she grumbled.

"It's not easy pulling the trigger for the first time," Shane assured her. She looked at him as Shane continued, "I remember the first time I killed. I ran along the edge of this high mountain cliff, and just over on the other side was this Korean kid. He couldn't have been more than seventeen or eighteen years old. He wore the enemy's uniform, carried the enemy's rifle, but I swear to this day he was just a civilian boy caught up in the middle of the war."

"What happened then?" Angel inquired as she had rarely heard him talk about his deployment to Korea.

"He raised his weapon," Shane stared off in the distance. Angel didn't press him for more details. She knew it had to have been difficult for him. "The next day I found out that the kid had been the North Korean Army Chief of Staff's only son."

Shane still couldn't get the images of the boy out of his mind. He wasn't particularly religious, but before the Cataclysm he and Angel had often taken the kids to church on Sundays. He closed his eyes and quietly said a prayer for the dead young man. "You OK baby?" his wife said soothingly after a brief pause.

"Yeah, just a rough day," he looked at her with a forced smile.

"No, really?" she replied half-jokingly. "It'll be OK, we'll get him," she tried to comfort him. But Shane's smile turned into a frown as he wondered just how many blameless people would have to die before he could finish off the maniac. The doomsayer had shot him, and even though his weapon hadn't done any damage, Shane had never been shot or shot at without returning fire and bringing down his enemy.

Captain Dyson was going over his patrol schedule and noticed that Lieutenant Hawk's squad had not reported in yet. They were an hour overdue and he was getting a bit concerned. "Sergeant Liedel," he looked up at the six-foot-eight-inch tall man standing on the other side of the table with all of the tactical maps of the city scattered about.

"Yes sir?" the two hundred twenty pound muscle man with the bushy beard inquired.

"Lieutenant Hawk's squad ... are they still out there?" the captain asked him.

"They should be sir, they haven't reported in to any of the checkpoints yet," the sergeant confirmed.

Dyson looked at a spot on his map that had a red thumbtack stuck to the southeastern end of the city. Looking at his watch he remarked,

"It's almost 1800 hours. Sergeant, if they haven't reported in by 1830 hours I want you to mount a search and rescue party for them." He pointed at the location next to the thumbtack where he had sent Shane's squad that afternoon.

"Yes sir," Sergeant Liedel snapped a salute, turned, and left the room. He had to bend a bit forward to avoid hitting his head on the door frame.

Sergeant Rob Liedel was a tall, but built man with a thick beard and a beer gut. He wasn't military, but had joined the Freedom Fighters that NARC recruited after his wife and two children were killed in an auto accident while driving through Detroit during the Cataclysm. He had spent days in an abandoned bar, drinking away his sorrows until NARC soldiers found him passed out with a bottle of Jack Daniels in his hands.

In the days since he had become known for his short temper and lack of concern for the innocent or those in need. In fact, after the death of his family he picked a fight with any and all who threatened him or got in his way. When NARC rolled into town he had joined the ranks of death squad volunteers, and eagerly fought the alien creatures that were determined to wipe out mankind. During battle he displayed little or no regard for his own safety or that of his companions as long as he got the job done. In short, as a death squad team member he was the ideal operative. Search & Rescue really wasn't his thing, but he would often find himself filling such a role. For example, he had come to the rescue of trapped NARC soldiers or reinforced their positions during a battle with who knows what.

Combat was Liedel's newfound specialty and he almost enjoyed it. An angry vigilante, he was seeking revenge or some sort of retribution for his traumatic losses. He hated the aliens for causing endless strife, but despised the military even more. They had come and re-established the rules, and Liedel didn't like rules.

Extraterrestrials and other such creatures didn't concern him much as long as they didn't stand in his way. To his credit, he had already killed a legion of lesser aliens. In fact, he had slaughtered so many that he had lost count, and they included everything from the smallest monster to the largest Reamer. Not surprisingly, his comrades had nicknamed him the "Slayer."

Sergeant Liedel was also a fan of heavy weapons and explosives. He often set out with the substantial, rapid fire NARC GR-50 Grenade Rifle, which had originally been designed as an anti-armor and anti-fortification weapon. It was versatile enough to be used for riot control, firing either tear gas, smoke grenades or rubber shells. However, he never carried any of those on him. Nevertheless, if the human race was looking for someone to fill the role of a modern harbinger of death, he would be it.

Shane and Angel held hands while sitting at a round table, watching snow and ash falling from the sky. It was a blizzard of white and grey as snow drifts piled up to five feet high. It was also one of the coldest nights they'd experienced thus far, and the icy air stung their cheeks. Watching their breaths as they exhaled was a testament to their misery. Shane's nose was flushed red and he had a bit of a sniffle. Trying to keep warm, he had one arm stretched behind his wife's shoulders.

Angel was shivering, but comfortable in her husband's company. These last few hours had been quiet as nothing stirred in the neighborhood. Night had fallen, and what little light emanated from other sections of the city dimly lit the street outside the café with a faint, orange tint. Harris, Marshal, and Almazan were all asleep, while Mr. and Mrs. Hawk were about to doze off in a booth.

Suddenly, everyone shot up, eyes wide open and alert as an explosion rocked the café. The glow of flames was reflected in the windowpanes of a building across the street. Shane slid out of the booth and snatched his rifle from the tabletop. He put his helmet on as the others got up and started checking their weapons.

Sneaking over to a window at the front of the store, he slowly poked his head out the broken frame to see what was going on. He saw a large crowd of people moving up the road from the burned down church. The mob smashed everything that was not nailed down such as doors and windows as they surged towards to the café.

Shane retreated back inside, "Rioters are moving towards us. Get ready to defend yourselves," he told his squad. Nobody had brought any riot control gear, however, and Shane also wanted to avoid unnecessary bloodshed. The throng was half a block away when another explosion rocked the café. This one was more powerful than the first as gun fire rang out and bullets bounced off buildings on both sides of the street.

The few intact glass windows shattered as the mad crowd took random pot shots. Yelling and screaming could be heard as they set everything on fire in a frenzy of destruction. One jeering man threw sticks of dynamite underneath the gas tanks of broken-down vehicles parked on the side of the road.

Shane and his squad saw a Molotov cocktail with a burning wick fly into a nearby, open shop window. It detonated after a second, sending clouds of debris and smoke into the air and into the coffee shop.

"We gotta get outta here," Angel pleaded with her husband. Shane agreed and signaled the rest of his men to move along the outer wall of the building. Sneaking past the entrance, he propped himself against the bricks, aiming his rifle towards the crazed horde. The squad wasn't noticed as they stealthily tiptoed outside. A battered pickup truck with a missing rear tire was stuck against a telephone pole on the corner of the street and Shane hoped that it could provide them with some additional cover.

Almazan made a quick run for it, hiding behind the engine block. Unfortunately, he was noticed and Shane watched an angry rioter pointing at him through the sight on his rifle. Some folks in the crowd carried older weapons, while a few others actually boasted more serious fire power that was normally exclusive to NARC troops. Shane knew that those were the weapons that could hurt or kill them. A madman with a semi-automatic assault rifle—a relic of the twentieth century—aimed at the dilapidated pickup and fired a burst of rounds at Almazan. Some punctured the thin aluminum shell of the vehicle, while Almazan tried to conceal himself as best he could from the deranged mob.

Meanwhile, Harris had taken a smoke grenade from his pouch, pulled the pin, and let go of the safety lever. He threw the grenade and its cylinder landed in the middle of the street. The spoon immediately popped off the top, creating a huge plume of smoke that quickly filled the area.

Shane gave the hand signal to move yet again, prompting Marshal and Harris to make a dash for the rear of the vehicle where Almazan was extending the bipod legs on his M450C machine gun. Carefully placing his rifle on the hood, he waited for an attacker to rush through the smoke screen. By now, Shane and Angel had also joined them and were taking up positions near the pick-up's truck bed. It didn't offer much protection, but it was something.

Moments later, the lunatics' silhouettes emerged through the haze. As they cautiously approached, Shane and the others switched their weapons from safe to fire. One of the screwballs immediately discharged his rifle at the truck, but the laser dart missed the vehicle by inches. In response, Harris flung himself on the hood and returned fire with his sniper rifle. The laser beam struck the man in the chest and knocked him down, but he eventually got back on his feet.

"They must be wearing armor!" Shane's brother yelled as he squatted behind the vehicle again. Shane peeked over the truck's hood at the rioters, realizing that some were indeed wearing body armor.

Seconds later, more men came into his view, weapons blazing. Bullets and lasers struck the old pick-up, ripping the front side apart. Almazan now took careful aim and fired a short burst of rounds at one assailant. The projectiles hit and blew through the man's light armored vest with ease, killing him in an instant.

Furious, a whole gang of beweaponed hellions now charged through the fumes, gunning wildly for Shane's squad. A hail of bullets and lasers showered the old vehicle, although some missed. Growing desperate, Shane pulled his M19A2 pistol from its holster and handed it to his brother. "What's this for?" Marshal looked at the puny weapon.

"Your cannon will cause too much collateral damage. Use that, try to be more accurate and try not to kill any of them," Shane explained.

Shaking his head in frustration, Marshal took the revolver and leaned over the truck bed. He fired a round at a rioter, but missed. "Everyone hear that? Try not to kill them! Non-lethal shots only!" Shane shouted over the gunfire.

"Yeah! Tell them that!" Almazan shouted as bullets bounced off the hood near his head.

By now, Angel was taking aim at the crowd after Marshal had ducked for cover. She launched a single round at one of the men holding a laser rifle. It struck him squarely in the forehead, causing his head to disintegrate into red mist. Satisfied, Angel plunged behind the pick-up again, only to face an angry Shane. "I said no kill shots!" he yelled at her.

But she only shrugged. At this point, Angel did not care. As far as she was concerned, the enemy was armed and dangerous. It was a situation of "Us versus Them" and she wanted to see her children again.

There was no time to argue, however, because a group of a dozen firebrands materialized from the debris cloud. Taking up positions behind abandoned cars or inside shops, they fired a rain of rounds at Shane's huddled squad. Then, a lone individual rushed towards their hiding place. His heart missed a beat as Shane recognized the old, grizzly maniac from the church who had shot him earlier that evening. Laughing hysterically, the man lit the fuse of a nitroglycerin pipe and threw it at them. The tube landed just short of the vehicle and luckily Shane spotted it.

"Everyone down!" he yelled and covered his wife with his body just as she was getting ready to take another shot. Seconds later the makeshift bomb exploded, rocking the pick-up truck. The blast sent dirt, ash, and debris flying everywhere, and the squad felt the concussive wave of the detonation blow towards them from underneath the vehicle. Billowing smoke and dirt engulfed everyone, making it very hard to see anything. Not only was their vision blurred. If it hadn't been for their reinforced helmets,

Shane's men might have been deafened as well.

A few minutes later, after the effects of the shock wave had worn off, Shane popped up and fired a burst of rounds at the old man. Once again, he wasn't hit and simply vanished. Annoyed, Shane crouched behind the pick-up as muzzle flashes lit up the inside of a shop where one of the zealots had taken cover.

Now Almazan unleashed a long burst of rounds at the individual hiding in the nearby building. Unsure if he had hit the man, he quickly dove behind the vehicle.

At the same time Harris leaned forward, launching his laser at another man. The beam hit its target in the throat and burned a hole right through the back of the man's neck. He staggered backwards, gagging and clutching his exposed esophagus.

"Hey! I said no kill shots!" Shane was furious with his team.

"Hey! It's either us or them!" Angel shouted back defiantly. Meanwhile, Marshal was lying down on the ground. He aimed his pistol at an approaching individual and squeezed the trigger. The round narrowly missed his moving target, prompting him to fire again—in vain. A third round finally struck his adversary in the arm. The man fell down and dropped his weapon, holding his injured limb.

In the meantime, Angel had almost become the victim of a close encounter. She had warily left her spot after noticing a muzzle flash behind the corner of a building and returned fire. Bullets almost immediately riddled the truck right next to her position, while one glanced off the side of her helmet.

Angel quickly flung herself behind the vehicle, checking her helmet for entry marks. Luckily, there was only a deep scratch. Shivering, she looked at her husband who quickly checked her head gear. By now, Angel was crying quietly. "You're ok baby, it glanced off," he hugged her tightly. But Angel was still in shock and just sat there, motionless.

Growing concerned, Shane let her go and peered down the road. In the opposite direction of the church he spotted three sets of headlights coming towards them. Although they were still a mile away, Shane recognized this specific type of headlight as NARC military issue. He thought to himself, "It's about time!" and then shouted over the gunfire, "We got help!"

Almazan had gotten up again and fired his weapon at another target hiding behind a dumpster. The rounds blew giant, gaping holes through the large bin and he saw the attacker slump across it. The sergeant knew he had gotten a kill when the dumpster stopped moving.

Kneeling, Harris wobbled to the opposite side of Almazan's position. At the front corner of the truck he could get a better view of the street and soon spotted a man on top of a nearby roof. Pointing his sniper rifle, Shane's brother took careful aim and set his cross-hairs on the rioter's head. He released the trigger, letting the laser beam strike its target at the speed of light and with deadly accuracy.

Meanwhile, Marshal had found himself another target. One of the old man's followers was running across the street to another firing position and was squeezing off rounds at him. Each one missed, however, as the rioter dashing across the road was not a good enough shot while moving. He swore and smashed his hand into the ash and snow-covered ground in frustration.

Although scared, Angel mustered the courage to take aim over the truck's roof once more. She fired another burst of 5.56 millimeter sabot rounds at an assailant hiding behind the corner of the building that she had tackled before. A split second later, after she had crouched back down, gunfire from her adversary's position rattled the bed of the truck. "Shane, we gotta get out of here!" she yelled.

In response, Shane jumped up and laid down covering fire as his wife dashed to the street corner, seeking the safety of a building. Once there, Angel pointed her rifle down the street and also provided covering fire as her husband quickly joined her.

Almazan had watched them move and immediately laid down a wild spray of bullets on the road. "Go! Go! Go!" he pressed Shane's two brothers. Wasting no time, Harris took off in a mad dash to the protective corner as bullets zipped by him.

Marshal had also scrambled to his feet, but hesitated to follow the others as rounds were still bouncing off the truck. A pause in incoming fire eventually gave him the opportunity to run and he gladly took it. Projectiles zoomed past him, except for one which ricocheted off of his thickly armored, right shoulder plate. Like his siblings, Marshal made it to the safety of the corner building virtually unscathed.

By now, Angel had backed away from her position and pressed a button on the M71 magazine well, dropping the empty magazine out of the butt stock. Shane took her place and fired another long burst of rounds at different enemy hideouts. His offensive gave Almazan enough time to grab his weapon and sprint over to his squad mates.

A few brave, but deluded souls peeked up and fired at him, but missed as Almazan tripped over the curb and rolled behind the shielding corner wall. Relieved, Shane ducked as well and dropped his magazine. He pulled out a full one from the ammo pouch on his utility belt and slapped the magazine into the bottom of his rifle. Cocking the charging lever, he loaded a round into the chamber.

Upon doing so, Hawk suddenly heard an eerie sound. It was the hysterical laughter of the old firebrand again. Seconds later, something heavy landed in the truck bed and rolled around. Shane retreated from the corner, determined to shield his wife as the vehicle exploded. Shrapnel blew in all directions, while the pick-up bounced off the ground. A piece of flying shrapnel hit Shane in a soft spot in his lower back between the hard, matted plates. Gasping for air, he fell forward in pain. Angel instantly grabbed her husband by his chest plate and heaved him to further safety behind the building. Gently lowering his body on the pavement, she cradled his head.

Suddenly, the bang of several exploding hand grenades could be heard further down the street. Three vehicles were approaching the intersection with squealing tires and closed in on the attacker hideouts. Another grenade went off a second later, causing debris to rain down from an abandoned building. The lead vehicle finally pulled up to the corner where Shane's squad was hiding and parked. In the turret of the MHMMV Combat Gun Truck sat a tall man dressed in a full suit of NARC body armor. An extra drum of grenades hung from his utility belt. He launched another burst of explosives down the road as the second vehicle positioned itself on the other side of the street corner. The gunner in that turret fired a volley of plasma blasts from the mounted NARC PC-46 Plasma Cannon.

By now, a third vehicle had parked between the first two and its gunner released a long shower of rounds out of the mounted M3A9 .50 Caliber Rail Gun. The firefight only lasted a few seconds and then ceased altogether. Satisfied, the turret gunners relaxed a bit, but continued to scan the neighborhood for any remaining rioters. Terrified, those fortunate enough to have survived dropped their weapons and ran off into the night, apparently uneager to meet their Maker just yet.

The tall man in the first turret hopped off the vehicle roof and calmly walked over to Shane's squad. He didn't wear a helmet and seemed wholly unconcerned for his safety. Harris could see that his cheeks were flushed from the cold air which had whipped him mercilessly during the drive.

Suddenly, frantic laughter caught his attention. Sergeant Liedel swung around and saw a crazed, white-haired man wielding a pipe bomb with a lit fuse. In response, the sergeant calmly turned his weapon around, holding it by the barrel. The doomsayer threw the pipe bomb at the group of soldiers, but Liedel brandished his rifle like a baseball bat, batting the makeshift bomb and returning it to its owner.

The old man's insane grin turned into a petrified grimace as the explosive hovered in front of his face. Then he watched the wick burn out and his sizzling concoction detonate. Laughing no more, the old man was incinerated in the blast as three other pipe bombs attached to his belt lit up in fiery flames. The ensuing series of explosions rocked the entire block, causing the roofs caught in the blast radius to collapse inward.

Filled with grim satisfaction, Sergeant Liedel spit some black, nasty chewing dip into the snow. "Who is Lieutenant Hawk?" he barked sternly. Angel looked at the sergeant and then at her husband lying on his side. He was unconscious and bleeding badly. "This is him," she muttered, tears running down her face. "He took a fragment of shrapnel in his back. We need to get him to a medical facility immediately," she pleaded.

"All right," he agreed. "Is this everyone in your squad?" he mustered each of them. Angel nodded meekly and Liedel gave the order to depart. Walking away to the front of his vehicle, he spit more of the nasty black substance on the ground.

Relieved, Harris and Almazan carried Shane to the truck and carefully placed him in a seat. Angel was sitting next to her husband and did her best to patch him up as the other three mounted the remaining vehicles.

After five minutes of waiting, Sergeant Liedel climbed into the gun turret and tapped on the roof. His driver turned the truck around and exited the street that had brought death for so many. Together with Liedel's men Shane's squad swiftly headed back to the airport and arrived there forty five minutes later, without having experienced any further delays.

Chapter Two: Connected

January 4th, 2142

Lieutenant Hawk found himself lying in a hospital bed staring at a bright light bulb in the ceiling. He squinted and blinked repeatedly. His eyes weren't used to the light. Shane felt no pain, and he tried to remember how he had gotten there.

Then he heard a voice. The voice was gentle, worried, and concerned. It sounded angelic in its softness and sang his name. "Shane? Punkin? Are you ok?" After regaining a little more of his senses, he recognized his wife's voice. He tried to look around, but the muscles in his neck were stiff and made it difficult. His eyes scanned the room, but all he saw were blurry objects crowded around him. When his vision began to focus, the first thing he noticed was his beautiful wife leaning over the bed. By now, feeling had come back to his hands and he sensed that his right hand was being held. He looked up as she was bending over, kissing him on his forehead.

"Baby, I'm so glad to see you're ok," she smiled and looked into his eyes. He finally mustered the strength to say something.

"What? What happened to me?" he wondered. The words slowly left his throat and he sounded hoarse.

"You saved us," she soothed him. "You protected me."

"I had a bad dream," he mumbled and shut his eyes again. "The whole world was gone."

She frowned, pausing for a moment, "It's not a dream punkin…" Shane almost began to cry. He didn't want to believe it. Tears rolled down his cheeks and then Angel had to stifle sobs. "You'll be ok, just a couple more days and you'll be walking around again," she assured him. Shane sighed, but then the sedative kicked in and soon he was fast asleep once more.

Two more days passed and Angel was helping Shane walk up to a nice house somewhere near the airport. It was a two-story home nestled in the midst of a residential neighborhood not five minutes from the hospital, and a block away from the military's makeshift base.

She led him up a couple of steps onto the front porch, opened the door, and guided him inside. The house was beautiful and had all the furnishings of a cozy home. The lights were already on, while a furnace gave off much-needed heat. Shane stepped onto the hardwood floor, kicked off his boots, and then took off the long coat that Angel had given him that morning. He noticed stairs that led to a second floor to the right of the foyer, while a chandelier hung from the vaulted ceiling above them. Under the stairs was a wide archway that opened into the spacious kitchen. Shane liked the place. It was comfortable and peaceful, and reminded him of the happy days before the Cataclysm.

"So? What do you think?" his wife smiled at him excitedly.

"Is this our place now?" he asked, a little incredulous, and looked around. She hopped on the island in the middle of the lovely kitchen, pointing at two large windows and a door that led to a sizeable, fenced-off backyard.

"Yes, this is our new home. The guys helped find some furniture and things and moved them in here. We kinda had to scavenge from some of the other houses in the neighborhood, but we found enough stuff for all of us," she told him.

Leaving the kitchen, Shane inspected an adjacent room and took stock of a nice holographic vidscreen, stereo system, couch, lazy chairs, and a coffee table. The room also sported a nice carpet with the exception of a dark stain on the maroon fabric. Returning to Angel, Shane placed his hands on her hips, kissing her lips. "I love it," he smiled. "It's much bigger than our old home."

Gently pushing him away, Angel still held his hands as she hopped off the countertop. "Come on, let me show you the upstairs," she smiled knowingly and gave him that cocked eyebrow of hers. She led Shane up the flight of stairs, walking him through four individual bedrooms that she had designated for the children. A big box of toys and a desk with a computer awaited them in yet another room.

Then Angel opened the doors to the master bedroom. There was a queen size bed with two long pillows and layers of blankets with a down comforter on top. The bed frame was made of black iron, while the headboard boasted a delicate theme of silhouetted animal shapes. A nice, large oak dresser stood against the wall, and there was also a built-in fireplace.

Angel let go of Shane's hands as he explored the master bathroom. He saw all the usual appliances, but was surprised that folded, clean red and white towels were still hanging from a fixture next to the shower, along with a stack of towels near the Jacuzzi in the corner. He smiled again, excited. "I really like this place," Shane exclaimed. "It is much nicer than our home back in Fayetteville, North Carolina."

"We're getting power from a generator?" he asked curiously.

"A couple of days ago, NARC and several power plant workers went to the Detroit Fusion Plant, uh, Fermi III, I think it's called?" Angel waited for Shane to correct her, but he nodded. She was right. "They set up a massive security division there and restored power to the plant. And for the last few days they've been restoring power to the neighborhoods. Ours was second after they got the base connected," she informed him.

Equally happy to enjoy what were rare comforts by now, Angel went to the windows and closed the curtains. Meanwhile, her husband sat down on end of the bed. When he looked up, Angel was standing in front of him, smiling broadly. "The kids are all with the others, helping them move into a few houses down the road. They won't be back here for a little while," she purred and placed a hand on his chest, pushing him on his back. As she climbed up on top of him, they were both laughing. It was this romantic, passionate love they lived for.

Three hours later they were fully dressed and Angel busied herself digging through the kitchen cabinets. She had found some frozen food in the basement refrigerator of another house and was preparing to cook a nice salmon steak dinner. The front door opened up and the kids rushed in, followed by Harris, Safyre and Ambyr, Marshal, June and Paulee, Almazan, and finally Amanda.

Harris carried two cases of beer and Marshal a carton of sodas. It almost seemed like a regular evening. "Hey guys!" Harris called out. The kids ran into the kitchen and gave Shane hugs, welcoming him home. He thought to himself that he had already been "greeted" in the nicest way possible and smiled at his beautiful wife.

"Look what we found," Harris grinned and walked into the kitchen, placing the two cases of beer on the island countertop. Marshal put the sodas next to them.

"Oh, excellent!" Shane cheered.

"We thought you might need a couple," June laughed.

"Oh yeah! Crack that bitch open!" Shane got up from his chair and opened the box. He pulled one bottle out after the other, passing them to the adults.

Excited, Emily was the first to dig into the soda, while Jacob snatched one for himself and his little brother Jonathan. Harris's girls dug in as well with Safyre helping Ambyr to open the top of the troublesome can.

"Thank you Safyre," Ambyr smiled at her.

"I love you Ambyr," the older girl hugged her sister.

"Good Lord," Shane shook his head.

"What?" June looked puzzled.

"That's almost too cute," Shane beamed.

"Awww, is someone gonna cry? You gonna cry Shane?" Almazan teased him.

"Yeah probably," Shane joked back.

Madison was next to angle for a soda, but the following five were all intercepted before she could stand up on her tippy toes. Frowning disapprovingly at her greedy siblings, she was the last one to reach for the sweet, bubbly liquid.

"How ya feelin' buddy?" Almazan asked Shane and took a beer from him. He popped the cap and took a swig from the glass bottle.

"I'm good," he responded. "Thanks for helping Angel with the house."

"Hey no problem bro," the sergeant nodded. "You would've done the same for us."

Shane agreed, taking another sip from his beer. By now, the children had moved into the living room and Emily turned on the television. She flipped through dozens of static channels, finally gave up, and put a movie into the disk player.

Madison made another attempt to fish for a soda, but the carton was half empty and the last three cans had gotten stuck in the back. Eventually, one rolled forward and into her hand. She tried to pop the top with a proud smile, but couldn't manage. "Daddy, can you open this?" she handed Shane the can.

Shane paused for a second, replaying in his mind what his step-daughter had just said. He couldn't help but burst with joy and his eyes started to water. It was the first time Madison or any of the kids had called him "Daddy." Angel smiled as well, truly happy for the first time in many, many years.

He opened the lid with ease. Handing the drink to her, the little girl clapped cheerfully, her big, bright blue eyes lighting up the room. "Thank you!" she took the soda in both hands and scurried off to join her siblings.

"Hey boys!" Angel yelled into the living room. "There's a big box of toys upstairs in the den. Why don't you guys go see what's in there?" The children looked at each other like it was Christmas morning, jumped up, and ran for the stairs.

Jacob, Jon, and Paulee were already rummaging through the toy box when Madison trailed them up the steps. "Hey, what you guys doing?" she inquired as she had just sat down a minute ago.

"We're looking at the new toys!" Jon shouted.

"Hey, wait for me!" she hollered, set her soda can down, and hurried further up the stairs.

"No girls allowed!" Jon decided firmly.

Feeling unfairly excluded, Madison got mad, pouted, and called to her mom in the kitchen. "Is it OK for me to play too?"

"Maddy!" Angel replied with a raised voice, "Finish your drink first."

Already halfway up the stairs, Madison grudgingly turned around and eventually sat down to watch the movie that Emily had put on the television. She was bored with it the moment she walked into the living room, but thought, "At least I have my soda!"

Twenty minutes after dinner, Amanda, June, and Angel were washing dishes and cleaning up while the men were busy discussing theories regarding the mysterious energy distortion and how it all could have happened so suddenly.

Shane was holding Ambyr in his arms who soon wanted his attention and mumbled, "I love you Uncle Jay Jay." He looked at her and Ambyr cracked a big smile, clapping her tiny hands across her chest.

Angel saw them on the chair together as Shane laughed, planting a kiss on his niece's head. He made all kinds of funny faces and she broke out in a giggle. A wave of love and affection washed over Angel as she gazed at her husband a little while longer, marveling at his ability to connect with children.

Marshal was probably the most book smart of the bunch, but lacked the formal schooling to prove that what he was saying was true. "Dude, seriously, I think the energy distortion we're seeing is residual energy from the aliens," he pondered.

"Residual energy from what?" Almazan was confused.

"They obviously didn't come here by ship. So I think they must've teleported here somehow," Marshal explained.

"That sounds kinda crazy," the sergeant shrugged.

"I'm thinking that wherever they came from, it must've taken an enormous amount of energy to transport their bases and troops. But I can't figure out the primitive creatures. Maybe they carried everything on their planet at one time?"

"What do you mean?" Almazan questioned. "You're saying they teleported everything on their planet, except for the planet itself, *here*?"

"Sounds crazy doesn't it? But it might be possible with enough energy." Marshal concluded.

Meanwhile, Harris theorized about some far-fetched mystic expanse of the universe that had opened up the fabric of space and time. In his opinion, it all started with the eruption of the Yellowstone super volcano. "I think the cataclysmic event here on Earth opened up a wormhole through space and time, allowing the aliens to step into our dimension," he argued.

"I don't follow," Almazan reclined on the sofa.

"Space and time must've been jumbled up somehow, allowing the proverbial flood gates to open."

"Yeah, I don't quite buy that one," the sergeant snickered.

"Well, what do you think then?"

After coughing slightly Almazan speculated that the energy distortion was a byproduct of some experiment that had gone wrong somewhere in the world. "I think the government was experimenting with a new type of biomechanical technology, and the Cataclysm was the direct cause of underground nuclear testing," Almazan remarked, convinced he was right and had won the argument.

Harris chuckled, "That's more ridiculous than my theory."

"Well, until someone disproves it, that's my story, and I'm sticking to it," he laughed.

"So how do you explain the alien spires?" Harris shot back.

After a brief moment Almazan grinned, "I don't know, probably some alien engineer's design, overcompensating for something," he held up his fist, with his pinky bent outward. Everyone burst out laughing.

Shane started to doze off after drinking his third beer of the night. By that time Ambyr was already asleep, snug against his chest. As he faded away, Shane found himself in an advanced alien city with millions of human occupants carrying on about their daily lives. They wore garments reminiscent of the ancient Greeks and Romans, but bustled in a technological society far beyond his own. In fact, the entire city was a splendid jewel of architecture. White, golden, and marble stone works soared to much greater heights than any of Earth's tallest skyscrapers. It was clear that this society's engineering prowess was the pride of their civilization.

Stone gutters lined each sidewalk and flowed with crystal clear, pure water. And the city was clean, so clean it could only have been a dream or glimpse of paradise. Children played; adults conversed, shopped, and sold goods. Then, Shane found himself in front of a massive pyramid with a giant crystal onyx radiating at its peak. The entire structure was enveloped in a brilliant, white energy aura

Suddenly, Shane noticed that he was clad in a hooded, white robe with golden trim. Walking inside the ancient temple, he saw dozens of scientists and government employees who were about to begin an experiment on a new device.

A young, eccentric-looking researcher initiated the trial by pressing a button with little enthusiasm, while a panel of seemingly displeased community members scrutinized his every move. Then, crystal controls and blue-colored glass bulbs on the ceiling hummed and sputtered to life. Unsure of what was going on, Shane surmised that the machine was sucking energy into its vortex.

By now, the crowd's attitude had changed from skepticism to excited anticipation as the strange genius smiled, reading aloud the crystal displays on the device. Seconds later, however, his face grew grim for something catastrophic had evidently happened. The contraption shuddered, while the giant onyx at the top of the temple flared with energy. Then, disaster struck.

Shane looked on calmly as the community of onlookers ran from the temple and watched a government official berate the scientist, showering him with curses. Outside the shrine, a storm had already gathered. Lightning bolts flashed and struck every building in the magnificent city. But there was no thunder which Shane found odd. "Perhaps I cannot hear it, since I am inside the temple," he thought. All of a sudden, the situation deteriorated from bad to worse: everything around Shane vanished into nothing as the crystal onyx's brilliant light engulfed the metropolis which then fell into an ocean below. Thrown off his feet, Shane found himself in a spinning cloud that he could only call limbo.

The next thing Shane perceived was a dense, moist fog which encircled him. The ground at his feet was soft and wet, but something didn't feel right. It seemed as if he was traversing the bottom of the ocean floor. Only that there was no ocean! As he walked on in a straight line, Shane heard something breathing heavily, and a black object the size of a bus slowly emerged from the mist. He cautiously approached it and found himself staring into the eye of a large humpback whale that had been left to die on the ocean-less seabed.

Shane approached the helpless whale, and just a mere few feet from the creature, it exploded from the inside out. Shane raised his arms to shield his face from the flying flesh. When everything settled, Shane looked back at the carcass, which now had a hole in it he could walk through. Inside was black and eerie. It wasn't exactly what he expected from the guts of a whale.

He heard a muffled noise coming from the inside, and was too curious not to investigate. He stepped into the blackened carcass, and inside opened up to be the inside of a dark, dank cave. Very little light reflected off the rocks in the walls. The only light he could see was strangely familiar red angular lights spread out in the darkness before him. As he stepped closer, he looked up and seen two sliver white eyes glaring back down at him. "**I AM THYRION**" the monster shouted. With a tremendous force, the alien behemoth broke loose from the chains binding him to the walls. Rocks and flecks of water exploded all around the monster as it forcefully freed itself from its tomb.

He woke up with his name ringing in his ears. "Shane, what do you think?" Marshal asked him again. But Shane just sat there, looking at his family who were evidently waiting for him to say something. He picked up his beer, took a swig, and remained silent. He had to go over the images he had just seen in his dream and wondered about the who, what, where, why, and how. For some reason, he felt a strong connection between his mind's voyage and what was going on in the world at large.

Meanwhile, the conversation droned on with Harris expounding on his theories until Shane finally interrupted to share his new insights. "I got a strange image stuck in my head which tells me that some other race—maybe humans—developed the expertise to transport objects or areas to other worlds by means of a highly advanced device."

He continued, "These futuristic gadgets are powered by water. Therefore, the aliens must have used water, breaking it down to atoms which they then transformed into a powerful energy source. With the amount of water required to transfer their spires—which I'm guessing contain the devices needed to teleport their troops—they must exploit a planet's entire water reserves. Maybe that's why they came here. Maybe Earth isn't their final stop and we're just in the way. It might be possible that the energy distortion we're encountering is residual power from the teleportation process."

For at least a minute, everyone stared blankly at Shane. Harris finally cleared his throat and then fell into deep thought. "If Shane's theory is true, then it explains what I experienced before rescuing Ambyr a few days earlier," he mused. "However, it doesn't tell us how I was able to harness that energy into a physical force. That question will keep me up all night."

"And I thought I was drunk!" Marshal laughed. They all joined in and Shane smiled as he sat back in his lazy chair. He didn't utter a word for the rest of the evening until he said his good-byes when his friends and family left.

After putting the kids to bed, he and Angel cleaned up and shut off all the lights in the house. Climbing into bed together, they fell asleep after talking a bit about his dream.

"I heard what you said earlier about the aliens," Angel kissed him and wondered if he was right. These days anything was possible. It frightened her that all the recent upheavals might have been caused by an unknown civilization a millennia ago that had experimented with an energy force which ultimately destroyed not only their world, but was about to do the same to Earth.

"Do you really think it's real? You think some sort of apparatus invented by a culture long ago is sapping this planet of its energy?" she stared up at the ceiling in wonder.

"I don't know punkin, it was just an image that popped into my head after dozing off for a minute or two. Pretty sure it was the beer talking," Shane replied with a yawn.

"Well, I mean, suppose your dream is true? And that onyx thing was the cause of that society's disappearance and the draining of energy from that planet." She thumbed her nose, still staring at the ceiling, "Would it be possible that someone found the onyx and somehow activated it, causing all this destruction worldwide?" She looked at Shane.

When he didn't answer, she gave him a slight shove, "Hmm? Oh, I dunno sweetie. But how could the onyx have been found when it was attached to a temple?"

With that he tried to fall asleep again. Meanwhile, Angel continued to ponder these questions, speculating if mankind had anything to do with the Cataclysm until she closed her eyes and fell asleep too.

Chapter Three: Cleaning House

January 11th, 2142

The next morning was another standard patrol mission, with Lieutenant Hawk and his squad attached to Sergeant Liedel's "Renegade" element. At the beginning of the week, the remaining civilians had already cleared the neighborhood of all destroyed vehicles, along with the bodies and debris from the cataclysm. Some survivors still remained in homes in the area, and had even established a local governing body intent on restoring the community to its former state. Their efforts were thwarted, however, by a gang of rebels who brazenly claimed the area as their territory.

Inside a mall in the shopping district on the outskirts of the city, rebel gang members calling themselves the "Scorpions" had set up fortifications. When locals tried to clean up the streets with bulldozers and heavy machinery, they suddenly found themselves under attack from the rebels. Community leaders immediately requested NARC to move in and extract the terrorists from the area, prompting command to dispatch "Renegade" and Hawk's 82nd elements to deal with the insurgents.

The parking lot was on a slope that angled up to the entrance of the store. A three story parking structure stood adjacent to the right; a sparse strip of trees slanted towards a computer store outlet on the left. The parking lot surrounded the entire mall, making the buildings appear small from a distance. The parking garage blocked much of the view from the parking lot to the mall—a sizeable building with hundreds of shops inside. This particular area had not been too badly damaged by the cataclysm, and many of the glass panels fronting the various shops were still intact. Most of the doors, however, had been pried open by vandals and looters.

This was a good spot to enter the mall, the men decided. Six of the "Renegades," including Sergeant Liedel dismounted their vehicles along with Lieutenant Hawk's squad. Although they much preferred the warmth of the Combat Gun Trucks, they knew they had a job to do. Even the three feet of ash and snow could not stop them from carrying out this vital task. Shane stepped out of the vehicle first, armed with his trusty M71A2 assault rifle and M19A2 pistol. Angel quickly followed, with Harris, Marshal, and Almazan close behind. Divided into two groups, both squads met up by a side entrance to the mall.

"All right team, we're going to take back this place, with Liedel's team taking the entrance." Lieutenant Hawk started. Sergeant Liedel's firearm let off a salvo of shots, while the blast from his grenade launcher ripped the heavy doors off their hinges.

Harris quipped, "Now THAT's how you make an entrance!"

Hawk's squad laughed nervously, as they made their way, one by one through the back entrance of the mall. The power was out, and there was only some light creeping in through the sky lights and windows of various clothing stores.

With his hands, Lieutenant Hawk signaled Angel, Marshal, and Harris to head down to the mall's food court, while he and Almazan stealthily made their way down a long corridor of shops and stores. Weapons pointed out in front of them, Hawk and Almazan proceeded to the right, prepared to fix on any target that popped up in their immediate view.

Angel, meanwhile, led Marshal and Harris towards the food court, which was framed by a series of shops on the second floor. Light trickled into the foyer from a large, ash-covered sly light, and the smell of freshly grilled beef still hovered in the air. Whoever had recently been feasting here had left in a hurry as partially eaten meals and half empty beer bottles still lay strewn about the tables.

The small group cautiously traversed the food court with Angel taking the left side, Marshal the middle, and Harris on the right. Passing an escalator next to a two story clothing store, Angel started pointing her M71 Light Assault Rifle into each shop, eager to neutralize any rebel that posed a threat. She didn't find anything to shoot at, but jumped back as laser fire suddenly burned a hole into the floor tile right next to her foot. Momentarily stunned, Angel then dived for cover in a store.

Harris, aware of the enemy's position, opened fire with his SR-25, and quickly burned a large cavity into the chest of the first attacking rebel. Unfortunately, more rebels appeared along the second floor and the lower level near the clothing store entrance. As they began shooting wildly, Angel frantically keyed her radio, "Shane, we got enemies in the food court! We're under fire!"

"Roger, we're on our way!" his voice responded reassuringly.

Adrenaline pumping, Angel leaned out of the shop, fired off a burst of rounds to the second floor, and then ducked behind the protective store walls. In response, two sets of laser beams blistered more holes into the shop floor just as she ducked back in.

Meanwhile, Marshal aimed his MARG-3 cannon at one of the thugs, and squeezed the trigger. The man vaporized into nothing, as the wall behind him exploded into a brownish cloud of flying debris. The Glasser round had blown deep craters into the department store and the back walls of the mall.

Harris noticed an insurgent trying to move position, and swiftly put a hole through the back of his skull. Right after, an enemy laser beam burned deeply into the shoulder plate of Harris's battle suit as he was aiming at another target. Since the laser beam heated up his armor to an unbearable degree, Harris was forced to jump behind the counter of one of the food stalls.

Marshal took two laser beam pot-marks to the chest of his armor as three rebels opened fire at him from the center of the food court. Unfazed, he returned fire and blasted a hole through a large glass pane near the second floor entrance of the clothing store.

As Shane and Almazan ran back down the corridor, they saw Sergeant Liedel and three of his troops standing at the entrance to the food court, watching the battle. To their astonishment, Liedel then shouldered his GR-50 Grenade Rifle and fired a wild burst into the ceiling and second floor balcony, right into the rebel's positions. The grenades detonated on impact, sending thunderous shock waves through the entire mall. The ceiling began to crumble, and glass shattered from the sky light, letting the cold air, snow, and ash fall into the now open building. Furious, Shane ran as fast as he could and kicked Sergeant Liedel's feet out from underneath him – simultaneously grabbing Liedel's throat with his right hand and slamming him down onto the floor.

His three men aimed their weapons at Almazan while Shane pinned Liedel to the floor, "What the hell are you doing!? I've got men in there!" he yelled angrily.

But Liedel simply shoved Shane aside as the two stood up. At six foot eight inches, Liedel was a good head taller than Shane who was only five foot eleven. Behind the visor of his helmet, Shane's eyes flared at the sergeant, while Liedel grinned devilishly. Seemingly unconcerned, he turned away from Shane and walked back through the mall, followed by his two lackeys. Shane, meanwhile, was incandescent with rage, and had trouble restraining himself from shooting the sergeant in the back of his head as Liedel slowly vanished from sight.

At the same time, the rebels fled their positions in the clothing store as the walls and ceiling crumbled around them. Shane and Almazan were forced to retreat from the entrance as a dust cloud of debris suddenly engulfed them. After the dust had either settled or risen through the hole in the ceiling, the men took stock of the food court which by now was a scene of complete disaster. Slabs of concrete, steel bars, broken glass, tables, and chairs were scattered everywhere.

As Shane straddled a mound of debris, tears rolled from his flushed eyes and appeared beneath his reflective face shield. It was painful to take in this scene of destruction, but the emotional pain of losing his wife was even worse for Shane. Stifling a choke reflex, he began to scan the immediate area with his powerful rifle light for any signs of his squad.

"Spread out, look for survivors." Shane ordered the sergeant.

Together with Almazan, he scanned the destruction, but found no signs of survivors. The men carefully searched the rubble ten feet at a time when Almazan discovered Marshal's hand. He started digging frantically, flinging debris aside, and eventually found Marshal buried underneath a table and other waste. Shane joined Almazan, and together they rolled the seemingly lifeless man over. Marshal was unconscious, but the biometric meter on his suit still worked, indicating that he was in good health. "I'll stay with him, go find the other two," Almazan shouted out.

Lieutenant Hawk kept searching as Almazan began to call for a medevac over the radio. "Alpha One, this is Firehawk Three, I need immediate medevac support to the Southland Mall food court." "Roger that Firehawk Three, medevac on the way," came the crackled reply.

As Shane continued to looks for survivors, he heard something rustling in the wreckage behind a counter. Aiming his rifle at the sound, he suddenly saw Harris get up. Relieved, Shane lowered his weapon as Harris dusted himself off. "Are you OK Harris?" he asked his brother.

"Yeah? What the hell happened?"

"Sergeant Liedel lit up the place with his grenade rifle," Shane replied angrily.

"That son of a bitch! He did this!? I'm gonna bust him up! " Harris shouted.

"Later," Shane decided, "right now we're still missing Angel, help me find her."

"All right," Harris conceded, "but that jerk is mine when I see him again."

"Get in line." Shane growled.

Harris then hopped over the counter and began the search for Angel, while Shane canvassed the end of the food court. Suddenly, he saw something stirring from underneath the escalator. As he switched his helmet's visor from normal to passive night vision, one of the rebels materialized from the back of the escalator. The man was clearly dazed from the explosions, but held a rifle in his hands. Shane promptly put a hole through his head with the M71A2. The round punctured the forehead, ripped apart the brain, and exploded upon reaching the back of the skull. The man's body collapsed—headless—to the floor.

Breathless, Shane moved over to the left side of the food court where most of the shop entrances were buried behind small hills of concrete and debris. Switching his visor back to normal view, he felt frustrated, letting out a groan. Fears about Angel's safety crowded his mind. Every second he couldn't find her was one second less he could save her, he thought dejectedly, as he kept dredging through piles of rocks.

It is worse not knowing if she is alive or not, he realized, upset that he didn't accompany her into the food court as part of a team. He had always feared that something like this would happen; that they would get separated, with one looking in vain for the other. When she was by his side he always felt stronger, smarter, and sharper. Now, without her, he was lost and confused, while thoughts of her never being discovered pushed him to focus even harder on finding her.

Shane searched everywhere. He kicked over every stone, turned over each destroyed table, and was digging through piles of debris when Harris approached him. Meanwhile, metal creaked high above them and the ceiling shook. "Shane, this place isn't safe. We need to get out of here before this whole section rains down on all of us."

"NO!" Shane barked at his brother. "We're not leaving until we find Angel! Is that clear!?" Startled, Harris took a step back; he had never seen his brother so angry.

"Sorry bro," he mumbled apologetically. But Shane was still upset. They had only spent the last ten or twenty minutes looking for her, he barked, and he wasn't about to give up so soon.

Before the cataclysm, Shane remembered, they had fought so hard just to be together. Their families hated each other, and their friends considered them a strange pair. He was single with no kids, and she was divorced with four. She had wasted fourteen years of her life on a junkie whom the MPs locked up in a prison cell when they had arrived in Detroit. It had been a bad marriage: her drug-addicted husband abused her, threatened to kill her and their kids, and wasted every bit of money on his habit. In fact, he was clinically insane, as Shane found out when the man threatened him with a sword.

It was a relationship Angel had been forced into, and couldn't escape until she simply had enough one day. When he left the house to buy more drugs with her hard earned money, Angel covered her black eye with make-up, packed up the kids, and ran away to her sister's house in Fayetteville. Almost a year later, she and Shane met through a mutual friend, and fate took its course.

That was five years ago. They had been married for four years, and up until the cataclysm, it was the best four years of their lives. At first, she had been quite afraid of remarriage, while Shane's over-confidence almost broke them up. But their relationship progressed and flourished regardless, and after only one year, she decided to give matrimony another shot. This time was different from the first, however, as they held the wedding ceremony in the open plains of Glacier National Park in Montana. Only their closest friends and family attended, and they honeymooned skiing on the slopes of Aspen and skydiving in Arizona.

The hardest point in their marriage was when Shane deployed to Korea for a year. The North had invaded the South, but with their advanced levels of technology, the US quickly won a decisive victory. Nevertheless, Shane had almost lost his life during one engagement when an explosion rocked his convoy. Many of his fellow soldiers were killed or captured, and he was listed as KIA when another convoy discovered the carnage. The Army prematurely notified Angel that he had died in action, leaving her inconsolable after two uniformed officers told her the seemingly tragic news. She thought of killing herself a few times in the weeks that followed, but mostly drank herself to sleep.

While Angel mourned him, Shane wandered the North Korean countryside for many days. He was alone, outnumbered, and scared, but the picture of his wife and the children gave him the strength to find his way home, despite being vigorously hunted. How he evaded so many patrols and death squads was something he never told anyone, not even his superiors.

On a hot Sunday afternoon, Shane unexpectedly strolled right in through the front gate of his Forward Operating Base (FOB), to everyone's great surprise. He went straight to his tent, beaten up and dead tired, with only two rounds left in his rifle. After a lengthy debriefing with his chain of command, he immediately called home to Angel. She couldn't believe he was still alive and broke down in tears, sobbing. When he returned home and stepped off the plane six weeks later, she hugged him so tight that he thought she would never let go of him again.

Now, he wasn't about to let go of her either. Combing through the rubble, he was even more determined to find her, and opted to ignore regulations about maintaining silence by calling out her name. To hell with the rules, he thought grimly.

All of a sudden, an image of a previous mission came to Shane's mind, and he keyed the small computer on his right forearm to switch on his teammates' tracking devices on his HUD. Several icons lit up in his field of vision; three of them were Harris, Marshal, and Almazan. But there was also another one: Angel! Her icon popped up behind a mound of rubble blocking the entrance to a small shop to the left of the food court. Her icon was red while the others were green, indicating that she was badly hurt

Shane darted over to the mound of debris between the flashing icons, and called out Angel's name. He kept shouting for her again and again, digging feverishly for a way to get inside. He felt the seams of each slab of concrete to see if he could move it, but they were all enormously solid and heavy. Shane grew even more frustrated as he couldn't budge the largest of the slabs, punching it with his fist.

"She in there?" Harris's voice didn't surprise him.

"Yeah, she's in there!" Shane fired back as he slung his weapon over his shoulder. He grabbed the top of the largest cement block, straining to pull the top towards him. Harris readily gave him a hand, but even with their combined strength they couldn't budge it.

"Hang on," Harris panted, and ran over to Marshal who was still lying unconscious. He picked up Marshal's MARG-3 cannon, and detached it from his shoulder. It was large and heavy, but he was able to drag it over to Shane. As Shane moved to the other side of the concrete slab, Harris lifted the heavy cannon over his head, about to slam it onto the boulder. "No!" Shane yelled, his eyes wide with horror. "You could kill her!"

"I wasn't planning to shoot towards her," Harris explained. "I'm going to take a running jump with your help and fire down into the debris. The blast should clear the concrete, if I can angle it just right."

"If she dies, you're next," Shane exclaimed fiercely, while pointing a finger at his brother. He was shaking inwardly, terrified at the thought. In any other circumstance he would have never agreed with this foolhardy plan, but seeing how Angel was running out of precious time, Shane knew they had to move quickly.

Harris stepped a few meters back, while Shane stood ready, his hands cupped around his knees. Harris then ran towards Shane, jumping just high enough to place his foot into brother's hands which deftly lifted him up high. Boosted by his leg engines, the two men shot up thirty feet into the air. Harris aimed the large cannon on the target below, his sight on the food court's center. After he fired the cannon, the shockwave catapulted him another twenty feet into the air, slamming his back onto a low hanging mess of the ceiling. Harris lost his grip on the heavy field gun, and went into a free fall, hurtling towards the ground. Luckily, Shane was able to catch his brother in mid-air, and landed easily in the smoking crater below.

He set Harris down, and after the dust cloud had settled, both men stared at the giant crater created by the explosion. On its fringe, concrete fragments and pulverized cement dust piled up, blocking the entrance of the store where Angel was lying hurt. Fortunately, Shane sighed with relief, there was a small opening at the top of the rise near the shop's ceiling. He quickly climbed up the dust hill and peaked inside. His heart missed a beat when he caught sight of his wife's twisted body towards the back of the store, another heavy slab of concrete entombing her legs. She wasn't moving. Frantically, Shane started to scoop away piles of debris with Harris's help

Eventually, he was able to squeeze his body through a narrow space, but almost got himself stuck. When he paused to take a look at Angel again, tears welled up in his eyes. He could see that her face shield was cracked, and there was a large dent on the top right side of her helmet. Her uniform was torn and disheveled. She was just lying there, helpless and still.

"Angel!" he yelled. She still didn't move. "Hang on baby, I'm coming!" he shouted, wiggling his way through the tunnel-like opening. He had to brace himself on the other side of the mound when jagged metal bars, sticking out from the rubble, barricaded his way. Some of them were still embedded in the concrete blocks that had crashed down from the ceiling. As Shane struggled, he grew more frustrated. "Screw it!" he screamed, pinched in near a wall. Fortunately, he still had the use of his right forearm which enabled him to fire all three barrels from the cannons. The resulting blast blew away the remaining rubble, and he was now in reach of his wife.

After clearing these final hurdles, Shane recklessly slid down the slope of debris and raced over to Angel's side. He knelt beside her, took off his helmet, and placed his weapon next to her. With his right hand, he quickly checked for a pulse. It was weak, but she was still alive. Hearing a noise, Shane looked back towards the opening in the debris mound and watched Harris trying to squeeze through the narrow gap. "Harris! Go get help!" he shouted, beside himself with worry.

Harris darted off without hesitation, while Shane started to brush off dust, concrete fragments, and strands of rebar from Angel's body. Her first aid kit was behind her in the dirt, and he hurriedly unzipped the top of the bag, searching for the Portable Field X-Ray Scanner.

It was a small black and silver cylinder about ten inches long and an inch thick with a radiological warning sticker on one end. A control tab ran along its length which he pulled out. Shane then unrolled a thin orange plastic sheet made of a silky, translucent material attached to both the cylinder and the control tab. The tab was the controller, and he activated the device by pushing one of the small buttons on it.

He spread it over her lifeless form, looking through the clear plastic sheet as it came to life, scanning his wife's body. Shane viewed the changing images of Angel's insides as he moved the device around. Set on "bone structure display," he immediately recognized the compound fracture in her right leg. Angel's left leg was in even worse condition as the bones had been pulverized. Nothing else was broken though.

Shane then programmed the little machine to scan for tissue damage, and examined his wife's body for a second time. There were many lacerations on her left leg and a few on her right. He also discovered a small cut on her forehead. Finally, he set the gadget to check Angel's vitals. After a minute, a pop-up graph showed that her heart rate was very low, only twenty-five beats per minute. Then, just as he was about to put the scanner away, it displayed an ominous warning message, announcing an irregularity in Angel's health status. Shane was at a loss as how to interpret this information, since he had only used the scanner for quick combat field assessments in the past. His hands trembling, Shane switched the device to the unfamiliar "internal organ damage check mode." As he hovered the display over her stomach and waist, Shane broke out in cold sweat. "Oh my God," he groaned. He immediately jumped up, ran to the small wall opening, and screamed "MEDIC!!!" at the top of his lungs.

His adrenaline surging, Shane sat down beside Angel, and carefully removed her helmet. He propped her up, positioned himself behind her, all the while taking care not to move her legs. Cradling his wife in his arms, he reached into the medical kit until he felt a package of alcohol wipes. He tenderly wiped the blood from her forehead and her cheek, brushing her hair back from her face with his bare hand. She stirred a little and even tilted her head, although her breathing was shallow. Softly moaning, her eyes fluttered open as she strained to look up and talk to him. She tried again and again, and was finally able to muster enough strength to whisper almost inaudibly, "I love you."

With waves of despair washing over him, Shane began to cry hard as her head fell back into his arms. "Baby? Baby, no," he sobbed. "Don't leave me," Shane begged, tears streaming from his eyes. Enveloped in grief, he lost all sense of time, and didn't even notice a team of engineers making their way through the debris tunnel from the entrance of the store. Two men in rescue gear suddenly clambered through the small opening with a stretcher as the engineers cleared a hole large enough for them to squeeze through. They removed the concrete slab from Angel's legs, gently pried his arms from her body, and placed her on a stretcher. One of the men also put her in a neck restraint and bandaged her visible wounds.

Shane slowly got up on his feet as feeling surged back into him. He picked up his rifle and both of their helmets as the two medics slid Angel through the makeshift tunnel into the destroyed food court. From there, they rushed her out of the mall to an awaiting B-33 Fanjet. They put her inside the back of the vehicle, but told a crestfallen Shane that there wasn't enough room for him to accompany them. Instead, Shane rounded up Harris and Almazan, and together they followed behind in the Combat Gun Truck. Marshal was placed in another vehicle which trailed their gun truck.

Within fifteen minutes, they arrived at a hospital just outside Detroit Metro Airport. Medics and nurses poured out of the building, extracted Angel from the B-33, and sped her right into surgery. Shane, Harris, and Almazan were right behind them, although a doctor quickly stopped the men from entering the operating room. "But that's my wife!" Shane shouted as he tried to skirt around the doctor. He was stopped in his tracks.

"You can't go in there, Sir. Let us do our jobs," the doctor commanded firmly.

Shane looked the woman right in the eyes and fumed, "Then get in there, and get to it!" Her name was Rodgers, he read on her name tag, and after he had collected himself a bit, she asked them to wait in the waiting room.

Three impatient hours later, June, Harris, Safyre, Ambyr, Emily, Jake, Jon, and Madison came into the waiting room. Shane was still in tears, since there was no word on his wife yet. The children sat down next to their step-father, sad and subdued. Harris and June announced that they planned to check up on Marshal. They walked out as Madison climbed up onto Shane's lap. "Is mommy ok?" she asked, her big worried eyes glistening with tears. When Shane failed to respond, still crying silently, she embraced him with a big hug. He shook his head to and fro, and held onto Madison as she rested her head on his shoulder.

January 12th, 2142

The following morning, Sergeant Liedel stood at attention in front of Captain Dyson. He was unshaven, dirty, and reeked of beer and sweat. Dyson, however, didn't seem appalled by this lack of personal hygiene, nor did he care.

The good captain listened to every complaint the sergeant leveled at Lieutenant Hawk, tapping his fingers on the desk. Meanwhile, Liedel recounted his supposed actions at the mall in colorful detail, while adding plenty of fabricated anecdotes.

"Sir, I didn't destroy the mall. It was in fact Lieutenant Hawk who fired the grenades and brought the roof down on his men," Liedel now stood at parade rest.

On the verge of losing control, Hawk wanted to beat the life out of the liar, but resisted. He merely took a deep breath and countered, "That's garbage sir! I don't even have a grenade launcher. This fool is known to use one, and was there with it yesterday. Why would I put my brothers and my **wife** in harm's way like that?!"

"Enough! Both of you!" Dyson was sick of listening to the pair. "You both need time to cool off, and you're both suspended for a week starting immediately. When you come back on the twentieth, I'm assigning Sergeant Liedel to your team," Dyson pointed at Hawk. Both responded in unison, "What?!"

"I don't need any bloodshed from you two. You will work together or you will both be gone. I'm also assigning an additional member to your team, temporarily of course, pending Angel's condition." Dyson sat back in his chair, chewing on a pencil.

"I don't need another person on my team, sir," Hawk was raging inwardly. "I'm assigning Nikki Besos as your medic. You'll need her until your wife recovers from her injuries," Dyson ordered in a tone that didn't leave room for objections. Hawk decided that it was better not to respond. If he had, he wouldn't have been able to control what was coming out of his mouth.

"Sergeant Liedel, you're dismissed," Dyson waved him away. Liedel turned around, opened the door, and walked out without closing it. It was his way of protesting Dyson's decision to reassign him to a team and a guy he didn't like.

"What jerk," Dyson mumbled.

"Sir?" Hawk shook his head, suddenly calm. "How is she?"

"She's barely hanging on," Hawk began to tear up.

"One more thing lieutenant," Dyson paused. "The man we arrested outside of Raleigh, I believe he's your wife's ex-husband?"

"Yes sir?" Hawk raised an eye-brow. "We had to let him go today. Military Law states that we cannot hold a prisoner without charge for more than twenty-one days," the captain shrugged.

"It's been that long already?" Hawk grunted. "Yeah, I'm sorry lieutenant," Dyson sighed.

"Shouldn't be an issue, sir. But if he tries anything stupid I'm not responsible for the outcome."

The captain laughed, "Go on lieutenant, go look after your wife and kids." He actually felt sorry for Hawk, and sad for the children.

"Yes sir," Hawk muttered. He walked out of the room and closed the door behind him. Putting his elbows on his desk with his hands cupped in front of his face, Dyson groaned and closed his eyes.

A few hours later, Sergeant Liedel stood in front of thirty men near an old US military helicopter on the other side of the terminal. The group wasn't lined up in any sort of formation, but had gathered around their leader instead. They were undisciplined, unprofessional volunteers that had already made a wondrous mess of things on the battlefield. Liedel had fought alongside many of these characters in the last several weeks. Every day new volunteers of the kind joined this rag-tag posse, seeking revenge or retribution for their losses from the Cataclysm.

Crude as always, Liedel started to shout, "I was reassigned today by that punk Captain Dyson. Sergeant Strickland will be in command until I come back." The sergeant's followers began to talk amongst themselves, discussing the change. "Another thing, as some of you already know, there have been rumors going around that certain people have acquired some pretty strange, unnatural capabilities. These human conjurors pose a threat to our survival. I have been given a direct order to observe them and assess any threat to the security of the local population." He lied.

"Screw that!" he continued defiantly. His men cheered happily. "These are your orders; should you see any of these demon worshipping clowns, you are to engage them without mercy. No prisoners. Destroy them before they destroy you!" The thugs hooted and hollered, fired up after receiving their new license to kill.

"Let's go hunting!" Liedel raised his grenade rifle in front of his chest, and signaled the pilot of the helicopter to start up the engines. He and five other individuals climbed aboard, while the rest hopped into nearby vehicles.

At about the same time, Angel's ex-husband Bubba Earl was released from the MP station.

"Thank you boys," he mocked the military police guards, rubbing his sore wrists after they had removed the handcuffs.

"Don't do anything stupid," one of the MPs warned him.

"I'll keep that in mind after I get my kids back," Bubba Earl grinned maliciously.

He walked out of the front door into the cold, ash-laden world, his mind racing. Although Detroit was unfamiliar territory to him, Bubba Earl confidently figured that he was going to locate his children. All he had to do was look for Hawk and his ex-wife Angel at the airport, the military's current base of operations.

Later that afternoon, Lieutenant Shane Hawk returned to the hospital where his wife was fighting for her life. The children had already spent many teary-eyed hours in the waiting room, along with June and Marshal. Hawk's friends Almazan and Amanda were also present, as was Harris. They began sobbing as soon as Shane walked into the wait area. "What's going on?" Shane asked bluntly.

"I'm so sorry brother," Harris told him.

"Sorry for what?" Shane looked confused. Then June started to cry. None of them had the courage to tell him.

Seconds later, Doctor Rogers came out of the ICU. Approaching Shane slowly, she asked, "Lieutenant Hawk?" Shane turned around and saw the young doctor holding her clipboard in front of her chest.

"Yes? Doc, how is she?" Shane wanted to know.

"I'm sorry sir, she passed away an hour ago. We did everything we could to resuscitate her, but she was too far gone. And the fetus wasn't developed enough to save either, I'm so sorry," Doctor Rogers said gently, placed a comforting hand on his shoulder, and returned to the ICU. She walked into her office, angrily threw the clipboard on her desk, and started to cry. She hated this part of the job.

Hawk just stood there frozen. He didn't know what had just happened. He looked at his friends and family. He looked at the kids. He couldn't utter a single word. Tears sprung from his eyes as his heart began to pound and his knees began to wobble. "She's?" he mumbled softly.

A crying Emily jumped up from her chair and hugged him tightly. Jon turned in his seat so that he would not have to face anyone, shutting his eyes. Little Madison also ran over to Shane, embracing him as he and Emily had fallen to their knees. They were wailing loudly. Jacob, meanwhile, was simply angry; he crossed his arms and didn't say a word.

There was also Harris who just sat there, hunched forward with his elbows resting on his knees. Marshal put his arm around June who held Paulee, who looked at his family sobbing on the floor. The little boy just stared blankly at them, unsure of what they were doing or why.

Chapter Five: Synergy of Troubles

January 14th, 2142

The funeral was held outside at Romulus Memorial Cemetery in Romulus, Michigan, five miles from Detroit Metro. Shane, his family, and children, along with every member of the remaining 82nd Corps were in attendance. Shane broke down between the twenty-one gun salute and the playing of Taps.

After the service, when folks began to leave, two black-clothed figures remained on the snow-swept field of headstones. One was Bubba Earl, the other a lawyer. As the kids gathered around Shane, the pair approached them.

"Lieutenant Shane Hawk?" the lawyer asked.

"Yes? Who are you? And what's he doing here?" he pointed at Bubba Earl. "Dad!" Jacob ran from his siblings to his birth father, embracing him with a big hug. He let go of him after a moment, smiling for the first time in weeks.

"My name is Carl Lunsford. I'm an attorney representing my client, Robert Earl Cane."

"What do you want?" Shane shot an angry glare at the two. If there was one thing the Cataclysm couldn't get rid of, it was attorneys.

"I'm sorry about your loss lieutenant, but we need to discuss the matter of custody concerning the children," Carl glanced at the kids.

"There's nothing to discuss," Shane put his arms around Emily and Madison, while Jon planted himself in front of his stepfather.

"I'm afraid there is, lieutenant," Carl replied coldly. "Michigan law, Article 2136.05 Chapter 8 Section 11b states that, "In the event of one biological parent's death, any children will be handed over to the nearest living relative—preferably another parent—with full custodial rights and guardianship."

"What?" Shane was starting to get mad.

"I'm sorry sir, but you are legally obligated to hand the children over to my client," Clark told him sternly.

"That's crap," Shane fired back. "Look around you! Do you see any government here? You do realize the world is in chaos, right? I will not hand over my kids to this douche bag," Shane pointed his finger at Bubba Earl and continued. "You are also aware, I trust, that your client has a history of drug addiction, criminal mischief, and mental instability?"

But Lunsford chose to ignore Shane's last statement, and merely retorted, "You're right sir, there is no more government. Consequently, the only active judicial system that remains is your own military justice. I will get your chain of command involved if I have to," Clark thought he had him.

To the lawyer's surprise, Shane just laughed, "Go ahead and call my chain of command. They're going to have a ball. We're leaving."

"Come on Jake!" Emily yelled at him. "I'm staying with Dad," he defiantly stared at Shane. "My *real* Dad!"

"No Jake! Shane is our true father, not him," Emily scoffed.

"I'm not going with that strange man!" Madison sneered at Bubba Earl. She had never met him before and always thought of Shane as her biological father.

"Me neither!" Jon buried his face in Shane's legs.

"Come with me kids," Bubba Earl ordered sternly. Except for Jake, they all screamed, "No!," sidling up even closer to their stepfather.

"Fine!" Bubba Earl yelled, angrier than ever, "I'll have your chain of command hand them over!" But Shane and the children had already walked away and were out of earshot.

"Don't worry Mr. Cane, the military will abide by the law," Clark reassured him with a pat on the back. Bubba Earl placed his hand on Jake's head, but didn't smile.

Hours later, Harris and Marshal were in the backyard of the former's new home just a few blocks from base, moving a couch from his white pickup through the back door. Setting it down because Harris wanted take a break, Marshal got angry. "Come on already! Let's get this in here and over with. We got a ton of other stuff to do. Stop being lazy and get back to work!"

"Jeez, relax dude!" Harris told his youngest brother from the other end. All of a sudden, a rush of energy surged through his body and immediately soothed his anger. He relaxed and smiled warmly at Harris who could hardly believe his eyes. "Isn't this the part when he usually bitches about something?" he thought.

"Marshal, are you ok?"

"Yeah, I'm good, let's get this couch inside," he said calmly.

"OK?" Harris was confused. Together, they found an angle, heaved the sofa through the back door of the house, and set it up against the living room wall. Unfortunately, Marshal's foot got caught underneath the couch, and he yelled out, cursing and screaming that it was Harris's fault. "Son of a snapping turtle!" he hopped on his toes.

Raising his eyebrows, Harris took a step back, lifted Marshal's side of the sofa, and let his sibling pull his foot out. Still fuming, Marshal sat down and took his boot and sock off to feel if it was bruised. Harris knelt down in front of him, "Let me see."

"It's fine, just give me a moment."

Harris took the foot anyway, massaging it. Again, his younger brother felt a current of energy pulsing through his body. "Wow, that feels great, it's not hurting anymore," Marshal cheered. "What the hell did you do?" Harris let go of his leg and both noticed that the bruise was gone. Marshal looked up and stared into Harris's blue eyes with a sigh of relief...and an expression of disbelief.

Lieutenant General Dusty May sat at his desk in the makeshift NARC Command and Control Operations center inside the Detroit Metro airport. He was skimming battle accounts of encounters with aliens, miscreant magic users, and rebels. The reports were getting old, he thought warily. Anybody not in a Battle Suit was hamburger. End of story.

Typing up his own report, he listed the number of losses that had been inflicted on his men in the Detroit River battle. Sixty two of his NARC forces had been killed, another eighty-five injured. At least we beat back or destroyed some of those alien menaces, he thought to himself. After all, they had annihilated thirteen Reamer monsters, one hundred twenty eight Squiddies, forty Asteryms grunts, three Asterym Shock Troopers, and one Asterym Commander during a clash in downtown Detroit.

Sixteen Asterym Scribes, thirty-nine Infineons, nine Manhunters, two Wraiths, sixty eight Zombifiers along with countless zombies, fourteen Nightstalkers, four Red Wing attack drones, and one Scythe battle-borg also figured among his tallies. Most of NARC's losses were accrued during night battles, he sighed, distraught that many more of his men would probably lay down their lives to fight the alien invasion.

The powerful Asterym were most common in the abandoned suburbs surrounding Detroit, and the toughest of these had been identified by NARC as the Odeon. A powerful Asterym Commander, he stood slightly lower in the alien hierarchy which included Thyrion, Havok, Shiva, Karna (deceased), Tiamat, and the twins Phobos and Deimos. Odeon and his class of warriors led the common troops when their leader or his henchmen were otherwise engaged. Typically, Odeon gave NARC forces the option to surrender before the start of battle or pay the price. Thanks to a few brave Magnums, this particular Asterym had been destroyed in a cat and mouse game lasting a few hours, but not before suffering heavy losses.

A sudden knock on his door startled the senior officer. Rubbing his tired eyes, he bellowed, "Enter." The door opened and a young lieutenant poked his head in. "Sir, we've got a big problem in Sector 7 Alpha," he reported nervously. May jumped up from his seat and the young, dark-haired lieutenant escorted him to a real-time monitor.

The scene that unfolded in front of the general's eyes was horrific. Sector 7 Alpha was a small town twenty miles outside of Detroit to the northwest. Surrounded by open farmland, it was being decimated by a huge, thirty-foot-tall Scythe battle-borg.

"It's a Scythe sir, and it's heading this way."

"Scramble the Valkyries, the Militia, and a platoon of Magnums," May tersely ordered his staff. "Take it out before it gets to the city."

"Sir, Sergeant Liedel's Renegades are already in combat with it."

"What?" May got pissed. "Dyson suspended him!"

"Yes sir!" the young Lieutenant responded. "He must've gone out on his own."

"Fine, whatever, don't let it wipe out that farming community," he continued, "That town is vital to our survival. Once the canned goods from the stores and supplies are all used up, we'll have nothing else to live on." His men understood, swiftly relaying the orders as May kept staring at the screen. The alien machine was on an all-out rampage, playfully smashing buildings. It also killed scores of civilians who had been running for their lives.

Thirty minutes later, ten eleven-foot Battle Suits darted through snow and ash-covered farm fields towards a smoke cloud, while the giant silhouette of the Scythe towered above them. The monster was in the midst of another killing spree, slaughtering an entire town of innocent people. Six Valkyrie Battle Suits soared overhead at a thousand feet and rumbling on the ground were nine NARC MHMMV Combat Gun Trucks loaded with troops and heavy weapons. They rolled into the devastated village, which seemed devoid of survivors. Bodies lay sprawled across the streets, some squashed, some torn apart, and others charred as if they had been cut down by plasma blasts. All were dead.

Itching for action, Sergeant Liedel let loose a burst from his truck-mounted grenade launcher, targeting the machine's vulnerable mid-section. As the explosives impacted, the Valkyries swooped down, circling the alien from behind while firing bursts of electromagnetically accelerated rounds into the Scythe's back plating.

Clearly damaged, the extraterrestrial reared up and let out a vicious, uncanny roar. If there was any sort of actual functionality to the machine being able to roar, it was merely for intimidation purposes.

For a few moments the Magnums' halted their advancement, their heavy weight leaving deep foot impressions in the frozen earth. Then the recoil dampening thrusters fired as each of the ten Magnetically Accelerated Rail Guns roared their own battle cry. The earth shook and the wind rushed forward as ten Glasser rounds ripped through the air at speeds in excess of Mach three. They tore through the creature's chest and shoulders, prompting black, oily blood to splash from multiple metal gashes.

One of the Valkyrie fliers unfortunately overestimated his piloting skills and flew too close to the alien machine. Snatching the Battle Suit out of the air, it squeezed the unfortunate human with its front leg claws. The pilot let out a bloodcurdling scream as his body was being crushed by the merciless strength of the robot.

Meanwhile, two combat gun trucks circled the town square and unleashed a series of sabot rounds from their vehicle-mounted M3A9 .50 Caliber Rail Guns. The projectiles blasted holes into the assailant's armor, but didn't attract much of its attention. The alien machine simply leapt forward and kicked the rear vehicle's side with its huge front legs, sending it tumbling into a burning building. The Scythe then grabbed the small Battle Suit and threw the body into the trunk of another truck after crushing it in its mighty hands. The impact caused the driver to lose control of the vehicle, and he crashed into a building about a block away.

Soon after, the Scythe spotted Liedel's Gun Truck. Focusing on the vehicle's pesky occupants, the alien's single eye shot out a beam of red hot energy. The driver struggled to avoid it, but the laser had already engulfed the right rear tire. The tire pressure burst the wheel hub and sent fragments of metal flying everywhere. Two of Sergeant Liedel's men were killed in an instant as the truck spun out of control and tumbled into a ditch.

By now, the Valkyrie pilots had banked around the town's outskirts at rooftop level, splitting their formation and departing in different directions. Their leader swooped up and back towards the Scythe, firing his rail gun at the alien machine. He struck it in the back of its head, but the metal monster didn't even flinch.

Instead, it spun around and jumped up, trying to snatch the Valkyrie Battle Suit from the air. Fortunately, the pilot flew a quick barrel roll and avoided the grasp of the large claws as the extraterrestrial fell over backwards and clumsily landed on a house, completely flattening the structure. The behemoth kicked up a large cloud of dirt, snow, ash and smoke.

Seconds later, another volley of sonic booms rushed through town. The Glasser rounds were overshooting the Scythe as it ducked to avoid another deadly Magnum torrent.

Rushing forward, it picked up the truck that had just gotten buried inside the building. In response, collision alarms began blaring inside the Magnums' suits a quarter mile away. Radar pinpointed the threat: a pickup truck was being hurled through the sky towards them. The vehicle impacted just short of their formation, spraying parts and pieces in all directions. Forced to abandon their positions, most of the Magnums zoomed away from the whirling heap of twisted metal.

Unfortunately, two weren't so lucky. A careening ball of steel hit one squarely in the chest and knocked his armor flat. The other Magnum was thrown to the ground as one of the large tires—still attached to the broken wheel hub and brake rotor—crashed into his left shoulder.

During these mishaps the Scythe took another burst of slugs from a Valkyrie rail gun, still unfazed. In fact, it gleefully watched the plummeting vehicle break up the formation of Battle Suits in the field to the east. Satisfied, the alien roared as the Valkyrie's banked away, and promptly fired another powerful beam of energy from its eye, disabling one of the Battle Suit's main engines. The motor caught fire and the pilot struggled in vain to regain control. In the end, the engine exploded, sending hot molten metal into the flyer's back and vital organs. He died before crashing to the ground. But that wasn't all. The hot flames had ignited the rail gun's ammo drum, setting the entire Battle Suit on fire in a series of sparks and fireballs.

Frantic, the Valkyrie leader radioed back to NARC Command & Control, "General, this one's a problem! It has already taken out thirty percent of our men and it's not slowing down! Request backup immediately!"

General May had been monitoring the battle from the start. "Roger Eagle One, backup is on the way!" he keyed the radio. Turning towards the young lieutenant next to him, he ordered, "I want Lieutenant Hawk's 82nd Airborne in there now!"

"But sir, he's suspended!"

"Just do it lieutenant, or get out there yourself!"

Lieutenant Hawk was at home with his children when the radio buzzed with the young officer's voice, "Lieutenant Hawk, this is Alpha One Romeo, over." Shane picked up the radio as Emily continued washing the dishes.

"This is Lieutenant Hawk, over."

"Lieutenant, report to command immediately, we have a priority one alert. Assemble your forces and contact General May ASAP."

"Roger, Hawk out."

Shane looked at Emily, who had gone pale and dropped a plate. "Dad," she started weakly.

"Don't worry Em," he soothed her. "I'll be back soon, just take Maddy and Jon over to June's house and wait there for me."

Emily nodded, "What if *he* comes?"

Shane knew who she was referring to and assured her, "Don't worry, June won't let him take you without a fight." He smiled, secure in the knowledge that his sister-in-law was overprotective of family and friends.

"OK, just be careful," she kissed him on the cheek and he walked out of the room.

Within thirty minutes, Lieutenant Hawk and his squad (minus Harris who had been called away on another mission) rushed from their locker room. Their newest member, Nikki Besos, was with them and she had just been issued the last female Firehawk Battle Suit. Loaded down with weapons and equipment, the group charged out of the terminal and onto the flight line. A C-260 Cargo/Troop transport waited for them, engines whistling and the troop ramp extended.

They were joined by forty other members of the 82nd that had come up to Detroit after the Cataclysm. It was a familiar scene for Lieutenant Hawk and Sergeant Almazan as they boarded the aircraft, because two veteran jumpmasters greeted them as they took their seats towards the rear doors. "Just like old times!" the old master sergeant yelled over the roar of the engines.

"Let's get this show on the road!" Hawk smiled. The jumpmaster pushed a button on the control panel and the troop ramp rose up from the flight line, sealing the paratroopers inside the belly of the large twin engine aircraft. The plane slowly taxied through muck of ash and snow, but the jumpmasters didn't even bother to buckle into their seats. Before the C-260 had even made it to the runway, they hollered, "Twenty…Minutes!"

Everyone on board repeated the order. By now, the heavy aircraft had turned to the center of the runway and was joined by two Valkyrie escorts as the tower gave permission for take-off. The massive engines screamed thunderously as the plane gained power and accelerated forward, while the paratroopers braced themselves for take-off.

June, the kids, and Amanda watched from the terminal as the large C-260 filled with daring heroes disappeared into the clouds. In a somber mood, the little group eventually walked through the airport and out to the flight line. Climbing into Harris' white pickup truck, they drove back silently to their new neighborhood.

On the way, Emily began to cry. "What's the matter sweetie?" June looked at the fourteen-year-old in the rearview mirror.

"I don't want to lose him! He's the only dad we've ever known!" the girl wailed.

"Don't worry. I know Shane and he'll come back. Really, if I didn't know any better, I'd say the aliens were afraid of HIM."

The aircraft rattled and shook as it braved harsh winds and turbulence above the clouds. The Valkyrie escorts couldn't fly as high and had already broken away and returned to the city. Meanwhile, the plane's pilots were one of the few humans lucky enough to see actual sunlight and blue skies again as they navigated around tall cloud pillars littering the sky. Still, the haze seemed to stretch into the atmosphere for miles on end. Also, the warmth of the sun's rays was short lived as they began their decent into the murky mists below.

The jumpmasters got up, gave the signal, and shouted in unison, "Ten...Minutes!" which everyone repeated.

"Oh boy! Here we go!" Almazan yelled in the noisy compartment.

"Haha! I live for this stuff!" Shane shouted.

"You guys are nuts!" Nikki screamed.

"Don't worry, you'll get used to it!" Almazan roared back.

"Hey Marshal!" Shane yelled across the cabin. "Marshal!" His younger brother finally acknowledged him. "Get ready for the ride of your life!"

In response, Marshal grinned humorlessly and gave his sibling a thumbs-up. He was about to jump from an aircraft for the very first time, and wasn't sure if he liked the idea or not. Nikki was a novice too. "Hell yeah!" Marshal eventually shouted, trying to motivate them both.

By now, the jumpmasters hollered over the constant roar of the engines, "Outboard personnel...stand up!" The paratroopers on the outboard sides of the aircraft rose from their seats, locking them in the upright position. The jumpmasters then gave identical commands to the inboard personnel, which was followed by "Hook...up!"

Each paratrooper now reached and attached his or her static line hooks which were secured to the left or right shoulder by steel cables hanging from above their heads. "Check...Static...Lines!"

After each paratrooper was properly hooked up, the jumpmasters beckoned, "Check...Equipment!" Everyone made sure their helmet was fastened tightly, parachute packs buckled correctly, and the pack tray's lowering line firmly attached to each individual weapon or Battle Suit. A moment later the jumpmasters continued, "Sound off for equipment check!"

Beginning at the front of the aircraft, each soldier slapped the next man or woman on the shoulder, indicating that that person was ready to jump. Hawk was last as he stood next the jumpmaster on the left side of the aircraft. Holding onto the static line with one hand, he pointed the other at the sergeant with an open palm, "All OK jumpmaster!"

The jumpmaster slapped his hand and yelled, "Stand by!" as the rear ramp door opened and an icy rush of air blasted through the belly of the plane. Hawk stepped forward, his heart pounding in his chest as adrenaline charged through his body.

A wall of grey clouds retreated behind the aircraft as everyone waited for the small, red door light to change to the yellow thirty second mark. It did, just as the plane bounced after hitting an air pocket and the paratroopers struggled to maintain their balance. But before he knew it, the light had turned green and the last thing Hawk heard from the jumpmaster was "Go!"

June pulled into Harris's driveway and shut the engine off. She paused for a minute, looking anxiously at Amanda. It was the first time Marshal was going to jump from an aircraft and she worried about his safety. "Are they going to be ok?" June finally broke the silence.

Amanda, equally concerned, looked away. "It's what they're trained to do, they'll be fine," she eventually reassured her. "One thing about Shane and Ignacio that I've noticed over the last few years is that they're very good at what they're doing."

Emily, Jon, and Madison had already left the truck and were waiting on June's front porch. Comforted by Amanda's remarks, June unfastened Paulee from his car seat, while Amanda walked across Harris's yard to her house after saying good-bye. June unlocked the front door, letting Shane's kids inside who were all clamoring for hot cocoa.

Meanwhile, as Amanda was fiddling with her keys, a vehicle pulled into her front yard. A tall, bald man in a black business suit exited the passenger side of the car. He wore a pair of slick sunglasses and was of stocky build. Trampling through the yard, he stopped at the bottom of the porch and barked, "Amanda Almazan?"

She hesitated for a moment, "Yes?"

The cold air freezing his body soon lapsed into a gentle breeze, while the sound of his parachute flapping in the wind was all he heard as he drifted towards the ground. After checking the canopy for any rips, tears, or breaks in the suspension lines, Hawk tried to get a sense of his current position. The ground was obscured by a thick cloud cover, and he could barely make out the other airborne paratroopers' silhouettes.

But there was something else lurking in the skies. It buzzed loudly, telling Hawk that it wasn't just a bird. Seconds later, Red Wing Asterym Drones attacked a hapless paratrooper by trying to ram him in the air. Hawk immediately reached for his M19A3 Pistol, but by the time he was ready to fire, the paratrooper's dark form was already gone. Shane frantically checked the haze for other drones or paratroopers that might be floating nearby. Detecting neither, he holstered his side arm.

"Son of a bitch," he mumbled to himself, cursing the extraterrestrials. Descending further into the cloud cluster, Hawk realized that he was approaching ground faster than expected. To his horror, a beam of intense energy suddenly cut across the air beneath him. Pulling his body up, Shane tucked his knees into his chest. "Ah crap!" he yelled as he was about to pass through the beam, which luckily had already dissipated into thin air.

A split second later, the sonic boom of a Magnum's main cannon assaulted his ears. Hawk's helmet muffled the noise, but it still stunned him. He felt the wind blowing at his back and reached up, pulling both sets of front risers into his chest. The parachute slowed his fall just as his feet touched the ground.

Shane forced his legs to go limp as he rolled onto his back. The shock of the impact coursed through his body, but faded as quickly as it had come. He caught his breath and then released the parachute pack tray from his body armor. Conducting a quick check of his Battle Suit, Shane was relieved to find that the jetpack was still functioning as were the electronics, hydraulics, and other systems.

He clambered to his feet and reached for his special M71A2 assault rifle. Pulling the muzzle cap from the top of the barrel, Shane brushed the snow off and slapped a magazine into the magazine well. A high-explosive round immediately locked into the chamber.

In the meantime, four other paratroopers had gathered near a fellow jumper writhing on the ground. Shane immediately darted over to his comrades. As he ran, he noticed a silk parachute about a dozen yards away returning to Earth without its passenger. The suspension lines were all cut and there was no sign of the unfortunate paratrooper.

He was sliding through knee-deep snow now, his weapon in his lap, "Sir! Private Bruzinski broke his leg on the landing!" Marshal shouted as the sound of rail guns reverberated in the air above them. "Stay with him! The rest of you, follow me!" Hawk yelled back and started speeding towards town. Three other soldiers followed his lead, and soon the huge monster appeared in between houses. It was trying to swat a pair of Valkyrie pilots who were making a nuisance of themselves. Several explosions went off around the metal beast, while one ignited near its back.

Hawk made it to a fence line and crouched behind a large farm tractor. He switched on his motion tracker which showed friendly paratroopers scattered all over the place. Most of them had converged in groups around various buildings. The majority were unharmed as indicated by green health icons, but there were a few yellow and three red ones too. Two icons blinked grey, which meant that the person had died. Shane couldn't help but think of poor Angel whose red icon had foreshadowed her tragic death.

Pulling himself together, Hawk signaled Corporal Lock to run to the nearest demolished wall for cover. While the Scythe's attention was focused elsewhere, Shane sent the next man forward. Private Panzica safely joined his buddy behind the wall.

"Dude, we're not gonna be able to stop that thing!" Panzica yelled as an explosion went off close by. Suddenly, the metal beast turned towards Hawk's squad, shooting an energy beam from its eye into the sky above them. They heard another detonation and saw one of the Valkyrie Battle Suits disintegrate into a fiery mess of twisted metal and flesh. The body then crashed into a field about three hundred meters away.

Another sonic boom shattered the air around them and Hawk watched as a plume of black smoke and sparks billowed from the foreign machine's side. By now it was a bleeding mess of metal, and let out another loud roar as a Glasser casing shot a sabot into its back. The Scythe hunched forward and fell to its right two knees, grasping a deep wound. "Now! Go! Go! Go!" Shane yelled, as he and Private Downes dashed for the protective wall.

Unfortunately, the alien machine looked up just then and spotted the two small earthlings ducking in their new hiding place. It instantly released a powerful energy beam from its single eye.

"Get down!" Hawk yelled and dove to the ground. Unfortunately, Private Downes didn't react in time and the beam melted his body. Hawk realized that the man who'd been running with him was gone when his eyes fell on a congealed spot of bodily matter. "Son of a bitch!" he fumed.

Ready to avenge his brother-in-arms, Hawk carefully aimed his rifle at the metal beast's head and squeezed the trigger. A three round burst launched out of the barrel and rippled across the Scythe's left cheek, right under its eye. The monster's lower jaw plate closed shut as it turned its fragile eye away from its attackers, while consecutive rounds still exploded on impact. Satisfied, Hawk joined Lock and Panzica behind the wall.

By now, the Scythe's body trembled as more troops fired their weapons at the ghastly creature. Glasser rounds from the Magnums tore off large chunks of metal armor from the mechanism's legs, while the two remaining Valkyries buzzed around the city destroyer like angry bees, firing slugs from their rail guns. By now, Lock, Panzica, and Lieutenant Hawk had taken up firing positions between two demolished buildings, and began launching rounds into the giant alien machine. Sensing that its end might be near, the Scythe raised its arms in front of its face to protect it from the multitude of projectiles. It took a step back as another time-delayed Glasser round slammed into its artificial abdomen. The bullet exploded, sending a geyser of fluids and fragmented organ pieces into the atmosphere. The Scythe screeched and staggered, but still failed to go down.

Hawk ran behind the ruined building, excited about having found a perfect firing position. But, just as he was about to pull the trigger, the wall in front of him came down. He ducked, showered by dust and debris. When the dust cloud had cleared, Shane saw Sergeant Liedel aim his Grenade Rifle at him from about a hundred meters away!

"WHAT THE HELL?!?!" Hawk didn't get to finish his curse as Liedel lobbed another grenade at him. He instinctively jumped and rolled forward, letting the device detonate somewhere behind him. Despite being inundated by more rubble, Hawk aimed his assault rifle at the sergeant and squeezed off one round. The Mach two round struck the barrel of Liedel's Grenade Rifle and exploded. The sergeant dropped the weapon and ran for cover behind another building.

Shaking, Shane keyed his radio, "Almazan, Marshal, keep an eye out for Sergeant Liedel, he just attacked me with a Grenade Rifle."

"Roger!" Almazan acknowledged as he aimed his M450C Machine Gun at the Scythe's rear right leg, launching a burst of rounds into the joint.

"OK!" Marshal responded as he tied a splint to Private Bruzinski's broken leg. Hawk now set the safety switch from burst to full auto, pointing the rifle at the alien machine's power source. He let loose a full magazine spurt of high-explosive rounds which ripped open the monster's chest cavity, tearing a giant, gaping hole into its armor. Then a laser beam cut into its right temple, while several grenades targeted its back.

Lock and Panzica fled their shelter as the alien machine swung its massive arm across the roof of a neighboring building. Broken chunks of wood and shingles rained about, but the men were already out the door. Lock sprinted to the right and then spotted Panzica trying to position himself behind the towering metal beast. "Panzica! Get out of there!" Lock yelled in panic.

But the extraterrestrial had already discovered the tiny human running beside it, and dropped to one knee. Bringing its mighty hand down on the unlucky Panzica, the Scythe flattened the frail human body in a hand print spanning three meters in width and nine in length. Then the Scythe got back up, bellowing proudly. A lone Valkyrie Battle Suit flew past its head, but was caught off guard as the alien kicked it violently in the chest. Flung backwards, the Valkyrie first crashed into the living room of a house about three blocks away, and then tumbled through a wall into a kitchen.

Furious, Shane fired another burst of rounds. As they ripped into an exposed internal organ buried deeply beneath the Scythe's twisted metal sub-frame, the monster lurched about as if drunk. The fluid loss also continued to weaken it, providing Shane with the much-needed opportunity to make a mad dash for the alien robot-borg. Dropping the first magazine, he reloaded his weapon and fired a burst of new rounds into the behemoth's chest.

The monster lurched around and reached down to squash the lieutenant, growling with anger. But Hawk was quicker. He ignited the boosters and took a thruster-assisted leap onto the machine's wrist. From there he jumped almost thirty feet high to its elbow. The metal giant tried to grab the disgusting little human, but Shane swiftly leapt onto the monster's other wrist. From there, he ran across its arm and jumped, clinging to its long, vertebrae-like metal neck. Soaring again, Hawk extended his arms and barely gripped the large spike protruding from the Scythe's lower jaw.

Seconds later, Hawk dangled from the spike, staring the metal behemoth directly in the eye. At this close range, he could see a large, organic eye glaring back at him. A yellow, transparent ceramic cap—shaped like a parachute-sized contact lens—sat over the eye. Dozens of tiny electrodes were linked into the ceramic around the yellow bulb, feeding energy into the light source. When fully charged, this electric eye released the devastating energy beam.

Loath to get vaporized, Hawk yanked the beast's horn with all his strength. It wasn't so much the earthling's weight, but the surprise that threw the Scythe off balance, causing its head to tilt forward. That put Hawk at just the right angle, and he jammed his assault rifle into the yellow bulb. The organic eye suddenly enlarged in fright, and Shane let loose an entire magazine of high-explosive rounds. The first round shattered the ceramic bulb, the second punctured the organic eye, while the rest exploded inside the extraterrestrial's head.

As the Scythe stumbled forward, Hawk let go of the spike. He fell and rolled under the monster's front legs, hitting the ground. Meanwhile, his attacker reared up and then fell onto its right side as black, oily blood gushed from its head. Standing up straight with his weapon at his side, Lieutenant Hawk watched the alien twitch as the dust settled.

Shouts of victory and loud cheers now came over the radio. The paratroopers gathered around the metal beast, observing their kill with the Magnums and Valkyries. Everyone celebrated the defeat of this incredibly tough alien machine. Luckily, none of the Magnums had suffered any notable damage, except for two that were slightly scratched up.

But before Lieutenant Hawk could revel in the moment, a powerful energy beam struck the bleeding metal hulk. The beam melted a hole into the alien carcass, and the energy gathered inside it. Shane backed away, just in time, as the Scythe exploded from within.

This reminded Shane of the whale in his dream, and what followed frightened him. He spun around on his heel and faced the direction from which the energy beam came from. And low and behold, Thyrion and his Asterym landed around the dead Scythe.

"**Puny humans!**" Thyrion shouted in anger.

Lieutenant Hawk raised his rifle but before he could aim and fire at the Asterym leader, a razor whip chain wrapped itself around his weapon. With one tug, Tiamat shattered Hawk's M71A2 into pieces.

"Crap!" Hawk yelled as the gunfire continued.

Thyrion swatted Lieutenant Hawk with his massive shield. And the lieutenant went sailing in the air yelling. But before the little human landed, Thyrion snatched the lieutenant by the throat and slammed him up against a brick wall.

Tiamat whipped her razor whip around in a beautiful ballet until she sent it screaming towards an unsuspecting NARC soldier. The razors cut across the man's body, splitting him in half.

Shiva smacked one soldier with the butt-end of his large staff, sending the soldier flying meters away, then spun the weapon around and activated the energy beam from the other end. The beam disintegrated the three bodies of the soldiers standing next to him.

The twins, Phobos and Deimos took to the air after the Valkyrie Battle Suits. Phobos fired his twin forearm cannons and struck one of the Valkyrie Battle Suits in its rail gun ammo drum. The drum exploded, sending the twisted Battle Suit crashing to the ground. While Deimos caught the other Valkyrie by the wings and ripped them off from the back of the power armor. The then helpless man in armor fell to the earth uncontrollably and crashed through a rooftop.

Havok located the Magnum Battle Suits entering the town from the east, he charged his weapon arm, and fired a single long penetrating beam of energy that struck the lead Magnum square in the chest plate. To Havok's surprise, the energy beam did not puncture through the tough armor of the Magnum, but did leave a smoldering melted crater.

The soldiers exposed on the ground scattered in terror. Some fired at the aliens in retaliation, but the Asterym warriors shrugged off their attacks like gnats.

Thyrion squeezed Lieutenant Hawk's throat, but the hardened matting made it more difficult than Thyrion expected to kill the little human. Thyrion took a closer look at the wailing human in his clawed hand. Something about this one seemed awfully familiar, and angered the monster.

Loudly, thunderously, Thyrion shouted at the tiny human, "**I AM THYRION!**"

Lieutenant Hawk watched the ripples beneath the gel sack as the alien monster shouted. Then he noticed the scar on the beasts right side of his face.

"I know who you are." Shane replied nonchalantly. Thyrion paused, almost startled, almost pleased. "You should know then," Hawk stretched his neck as best he could in the alien's tight grip. "That I'm the one who gave you this!" Hawk reached up with one hand, one finger extended and caressed the scar from the top of Thyrions eye down to his cheek.

Utterly enraged, Thyrion slammed the Lieutenant through the brick wall of the building. When the dust settled, Thyrion could find no trace of the unruly lieutenant.

When suddenly, a Glasser round exploded off of Thyrions left shoulder. The powerful round knocked Thyrion off-balance. And before he could regain his composure, Lieutenant Hawk rocketed out of the building with his 40 inch vibro-blades extended and jammed them into Thyrions chest plate. Swinging his body around and using his moment, the tiny human tossed the giant Asterym leader thirty feet away, crashing into the back of Tiamat.

Hawk landed where Thyrion stood and readied for another attack. But Thyrion stood up, shocked, surprised and thoroughly enraged, "**Asterym! Retreat!**"

The order caught everyone off guard, even the other Asterym warriors. Thyrion bounded into the sky, his boosters ignited, and sailed away into the clouds. Confused, his minions followed.

Almazan approached his friend, "I don't get it," Shane watched intently until all of the aliens were out of sight. "Why didn't they finish us off? They had us."

"I think I pissed *him* off." Shane muttered.

"Pissed who off?" the sergeant wondered.

"Thyrion," Shane dusted his armor off. "He knows who I am now."

"Is that a good thing or a bad thing?" Almazan shivered.

Shane looked at his friend, "It's personal now."

As the NARC and 82nd troops re-organized, jubilation was no longer in their minds. Although Sergeant Liedel was none too thrilled about Hawk and his men's involvement in this crucial victory. In fact, he was furious that Shane had stolen his thunder. Walking away in a huff, he gathered up the remaining three of twenty-four former Renegades and found a quiet spot to wait for transports.

In the meantime, Hawk reconnected with Almazan, Marshal, and Nikki. They were all unscathed and very excited. "Hey bro," Marshal exclaimed. "Now I know why you loved being a paratrooper so much, the jump out of that plane was a hell of a rush!"

"Yeah, no kidding!" Nikki added. "But man! That move at the end was wicked sweet!"

"I'm sure they didn't teach you that in basic!" Marshal snickered.

Shane laughed, "Nah, I don't know why I did that, totally reckless, but wow, it was almost fun!" he grinned. He was pumped, excited, and proud, and had momentarily forgotten his sorrows.

"It was like something out of a cartoon. You just scaled that thing with such little effort, well at least it looked that way," Almazan remarked admiringly. "And then pissing off Thyrion? That was just fueling the fire bro!"

"Hell ain't got nothin' on me!" Shane joked. "Well, I'm sure if Angel saw me do that she'd friggin kill me," he added. "So don't tell my wife."

They all went silent. Shane was more afraid of his wife than a thirty foot alien monster, Almazan thought. His comment also killed the mood. Apparently, he'd already forgotten about her awful death two days ago, and that bothered everyone.

For a few minutes the squad sat around and shared a cigarette while Lieutenant Hawk made his way around the battlefield, talking to other troopers. They overheard his colleagues discussing his move on the Scythe, awed and incredulous. "So what do we do now Shane?" Marshal eventually asked.

"Well, now we wait for a ride. Is everyone all right?"

"I'm fine," Almazan told him.

"Yeah, we're good," Marshal answered for himself and Nikki.

"Good. While we're waiting, we'll help anyone who's injured and search for survivors,"

Shane told them. "By the way Nikki, where were you during all this?" Hawk wondered.

"Um," she paused. "I was tending to the wounded. That's my first priority."

Shane nodded his head, "Nikki, walk with me, there's a few things I need you to understand." Frowning beneath her helmet, she got up from the mangled carcass of what had once been a Gun Truck.

Out of earshot from the others, Hawk looked at her, "I know you think you're a medic first, but right now our team comes first. If we're in combat, I need you to fire your weapon. If one of us gets injured, then I need you to do your job."

She looked confused, "Sir, those men are..."

Hawk cut her off, "No, I mean us, our squad. The other squads and platoons have their own combat medics. You'll create confusion if you jump in their lanes. While what you did is commendable, it's just not the correct action at the moment," he explained.

"For the time being, your only worry is Marshal, Almazan, Harris, and myself. You can help treat others later. Think of it like a firing lane. Stick to your lane, you don't need overlapping fields of fire unless absolutely necessary. OK?"

"I understand sir," she smiled. Hawk's explanation had actually clarified her role and responsibilities. "Sir," she paused before he turned to rejoin Marshal and Almazan.

"Yes Lieutenant?"

"I'm sorry to hear about your wife," she frowned. Hawk looked away as the smile beneath his helmet vanished.

Night fell over the skies of Detroit as bad weather had rolled in from Lake Huron that afternoon. It was snowing heavily, and June was anxiously waiting for her husband and brother-in-law's return from their mission. Staring out the main window with baby Paulee in her arms, she watched the storm approaching from the north and wondered if more terrible things were lying in store for them.

Meanwhile, Jon and Madison were busy playing games on the PlayBox 720. Jon was also teasing his little sister, laughing and poking her ear with a wet fingertip. Upset, Madison told him to stop and rubbed her ear, but Jon just smiled and licked his finger again. Unruffled by her siblings, Emily sat in the lazy-boy chair reading an Advanced Mathematics text book she had picked up from a high school somewhere in Virginia.

Suddenly the phone rang and Madison called out, "June! It's Amanda!"

June looked at the girl while answering the phone, "Hello?"

"June, its Amanda," she paused for a moment. Meanwhile, June wondered how Madison could have possibly known.

"Hey Amanda, what's up?" she asked quietly.

"Have you seen Harris? He left his house a few hours ago before the guys took off, and I haven't seen or heard from him since."

"Nah, I'm sorry, I have no idea."

"OK, I'm getting worried. If you see him, would you let me know?" she asked.

"Yeah sure, no problem."

"Oh, hey June," Amanda added, hoping she hadn't hung up the phone yet.

"Yeah?"

"Have you heard from any of the guys that left on that mission earlier today?"

"No, I'm sorry, I haven't."

"K, thanks," Amanda ended the conversation.

June walked up to Madison just as Jon was poking her in the other ear. "Jon, stop bugging your sister!" she scolded as the little girl screamed at him. The boy pouted, crossed his arms over his chest, and stared at the floor. "Maddy, how did you know that was Amanda calling on the phone?" June inquired.

"I dunno," she went back to playing with her video game.

"You just knew?" June asked.

"I just did," Madison shrugged with big doe eyes.

On the other side of the street, next to Harris's house, the jet black car was still parked in the front yard. Amanda was sitting in her living room, impatiently listening to the bald man who was going on about problems with alien hordes on the north side of town. "I understand the trouble you're having. But what does any of this have to do with me?" she asked as she set the phone down on the coffee table in front of her.

"What we need is a group of volunteers," he said gravely, "to undergo genetic augmentation to help battle these aliens."

"Genetic augmentation?" the term frightened her.

"We've been in the process of creating advanced and powerful super-humans that can subdue and destroy the hordes," he paused. "It's completely safe and there are no side effects."

"What kind of advancements?" she was curious.

"The kind that makes your skin as tough as a Magnum's armor, the ability to jump twenty feet in the air, punch through brick walls, and run at uncanny speeds without the use of a Battle Suit," he smiled, knowing that he had piqued her interest.

"How do I get my husband and me into this program?"

"Just sign at the bottom," he pulled out a folded stack of papers, spreading them on the coffee table. Amanda skimmed through them, asked for a pen, and signed the dotted line for both herself and Almazan. After the bald man had collected the documents, he quickly got up and headed for the door. "We'll be contacting you," he told her, no longer polite, and left.

Chapter Six: Iridescent

January 15th, 2142

Five feet of snow are hard to trudge through, Harris groaned, as he covered himself in a hooded sweatshirt and wrapped a scarf around his mouth and nose. He had entered an abandoned section of the city that was off-limits to all military and civilians. One of the energy distortion zones was rumored to be in this area and Harris was dying to check it out.

Peering up a crumbling skyscraper, Harris thought that only a month ago this building had been bustling with activity. Now he could barely make out street signs and lamp posts. Mounds of snow covered the sidewalks, and he recognized the broken windshield of a buried vehicle underneath the white mass. Hurrying along, Harris suddenly felt his body invigorated by the same, unknown energy source of a few days ago. He checked his watch; it was a quarter past midnight.

After rounding the corner of an office building, Harris finally found what he had been looking for. In the middle of the street, about a block away, the energy distortion that was cutting through the landscape across the globe sizzled and glowed, illuminating the neighborhood. With each step towards it, Harris felt his own powers increase.

Then, approaching ever closer, the force heightened his senses dramatically. His vision improved to the point that he took his prescription glasses off and placed them in his pocket. He could hear the faint crackling of energy amid the blowing wind and the sound of ice crystals shifting over layers of ashy snow mounds. Harris felt nothing now, but energy surging through his body and the cold whipping at his extremities.

As he stepped into the actual force field, Harris's body seemed to vanish, consumed by the potent sphere. He felt more powerful, younger, and sharper than he'd ever felt in the entire thirty years of his life.

All of a sudden, Harris heard the loud squealing of rats from under the street. He turned to face them, thinking that he wanted to levitate, and did so seconds later when three, dog-sized Alien Demon Rats sprang out of a sewer drain.

As they rushed towards him, Harris held out his hand. Lightning shot forth from his fingertips and struck down the first assailant. The rat's charred flesh caught fire and stunk, while its companions momentarily paused in fear. Seconds later, they flung themselves at the man floating in the residual energy wave. Harris held out his hands again and lightning struck both creatures. One died, whereas the other was so badly burned that it ran off, leaving behind a thick trail of oily, red blood and the stench of singed hair.

Electrified by his newfound powers, Harris floated down to the street and stopped by a pair of manholes protruding from the snow-covered asphalt. While steam vapors escaped from the small openings, Harris lifted the manhole cover off the ground, hoisted it in the air for a split second, and then hurled it through a large glass pane. Staring into the sewer, he recklessly decided to jump into it. All the while a Special Forces NARC soldier sat patiently at the top of a forty story building, video-recording everything through the combat camera on his SR-25 Sniper Rifle.

Initially, Harris could barely see in the dark, cavernous drain, but when he held out his hand again, several white vapor wisps illuminated his palm. The vapors clung together, forming a ball of gas.

Strangely, Harris found himself speaking in a magical tongue as the gas ball bloomed into a glowing sphere of radiant light. In fact, the sphere was so bright it almost blinded him. Harris also noticed that the globe followed his hand movements. Cool, he thought.

Trying to find his bearings, he didn't see anything at first. Then, a whiff of stinking, charred flesh caught his attention and he decided to follow the smell.

Nearing one end of the sewer, Harris observed that it dropped off fifty feet into an old, abandoned subway tunnel. In the corner, the ceiling of a square chamber had caved, leaving slabs of concrete, thick wires, and cables dangling in the air. Still bursting with energy, Harris leapt from the edge of a sewer pipe and grabbed onto one of the hanging cables. The globe of light fully illuminated his flying path.

In his early twenties Harris had spent four years in the United States Marines Corps and rappelled out of B-33 Fanjets. Now his muscle memory returned, and he slid down the wire with ease, planting his feet into the dirt-covered subway tunnel below. Letting go of the sagging cable, he knelt down and discovered tracks in the dust leading to the left. Stepping between the subway rails, he followed the underground trail.

The tracks dispersed as he came to a completely destroyed section of the underpass. Inspecting the cave, Harris realized that not even the smallest creature could have found a passage here. Stumped, he turned left again and spotted an opening heading even further underground. It wasn't large enough for a person to walk through, but he managed by crouching and crawling.

A warm breeze of air brushed against him as the passageway opened up into a small cavern. Then, twenty feet below, Harris espied a nest of

Alien Demon Rats chewing on human bones. Disgusted by the sight he wanted to electrocute them, but was unsure if he could do so before they attacked him. Just as he was preparing to turn the demonic bunch into rat burgers, he heard a female voice scream in terror.

Carefully sneaking along the narrow shaft, he caught a devilish voice speaking in a strange, foreign tongue. By now, the tunnel had widened and the ceiling risen to where he could stand up again. Petrified, Harris's eyes fell on a macabre tapestry of bloody, five-fingered claw marks splattered along both sides of the tunnel as well as the dirt at his feet.

Then, a large cavern resembling a great, dug out hall appeared at the end of the underpass. Pits of fire burned in all four corners, while dirt walls gave way to a smooth marble stage and paneling that extended over a hundred meters.

Harris gasped in wonder when he came upon a cathedral that had been hewn into the marble wall. There was no door, but a large, fifty-foot-tall rectangular opening. Within, a magical nexus of energy crackled with reddish-green lightning. The lightning flashes shot out from the center to half a dozen white crystal devices bolted into the corners and sides of the entrance. Above the nexus, the energy formed the fiendish outline of a pentagram which burst into continual flames.

A few feet from the magical doorway Harris noticed a tall, slender, dark-haired female clad in a long, red dress. Her wrists were chained to two ten-foot tall, black iron rods, and she was facing away from him.

Suspended from the rods just inches above the marble floor, Harris thought her some sort of sacrificial victim as her toes just barely grazed the marble surface. A group of men and women were gathered inside the chamber, chanting a diabolical tune.

Until now, Harris had only heard stories and caught brief glimpses of the monster holding court at the center of the room, but he immediately recognized the fourteen-foot-tall being. There was no doubt that it was Thyrion, despite him facing away from Harris. Lifting his massive arms, he called upon a puny earthling named Bubba Earl.

A man eagerly stepped forward, dressed in a black robe. After removing his hood, Harris could see that the individual was indeed Angel's ex-husband. There was also a boy beside him. Harris gasped when he recognized Jacob, who was also wearing a black robe.

What has that man done to that boy? Harris fumed. He wanted to rescue Jacob, and let Shane know what his father was doing to him. Unfortunately, there wasn't time for that. Harris couldn't fight Thyrion on his own, especially without his Battle Suit and weapons.

Weighing his options, Harris extinguished the light globe in his hand and dropped down on his belly at the tunnel entrance. He knew he had to think fast if he wanted to pry the boy from Thyrion's lethal clutches.

"**What is it you want, tiny human insect?**" Thyrion growled at Bubba Earl.

"I know the one who scarred you, Lord Thyrion." The monster roared and smashed his giant hand onto the floor. "His name is Lieutenant Shane Hawk. He's one of the earthly leaders fighting you."

"**Why are you telling me this human?**" Thyrion growled again.

"My Lord," Jacob's father paused. "He is my enemy too, and I am in a position to help you get revenge."

"**How so?**" Thyrion was interested.

"The children living with him are not his own, they are mine. His human commanders will force him to return them to me to a place and time of my choosing," Bubba Earl explained.

"**What's your proposal then flesh creature?**" Thyrion impatiently waved his hand.

"My Lord, I will set up a meeting with Lieutenant Hawk in a city cemetery. Buildings will provide you and your men adequate cover to conceal yourselves during the handover of the children," Bubba Earl brownnosed, never looking the beast directly in the eyes.

"**And?**" Thyrion grunted again.

"You may spring your trap, once I have spirited my kids to safety."

"**I like this plan of yours. I find it amazing how a species so physically weak can be so intelligent,**" Thyrion flattered. "**What do you want in return for your services?**"

"Immunity, my Lord," Bubba Earl humbly requested.

"**Immunity will only be granted if everything goes according to plan,**" Thyrion snarled. "**If Hawk fails to show, I will squash you like the insect you are. We will do this as the sun sets. Be ready human vermin, and make sure to produce this Hawk. Otherwise, I will destroy you. Now get out of my sight!**"

Bubba Earl bowed deferentially and scurried away. As he did, Thyrion briefly shifted his attention to the chained woman, "**You are of no further use to me. You will hang there until you rot.**" Seconds later, he exited the cathedral through a tunnel large enough to fit his enormous frame. Once gone, Bubba Earl looked at Jacob, who appeared brainwashed with a blank expression on his face.

"What a prick," he said to his incoherent son. "Now, follow me boy." Together, they hurried in the opposite direction and disappeared down a smaller tunnel. Left in the room were several other men as well as the unfortunate woman in the red dress.

With all his might, Harris held out his hand and focused his energy on the crackling nexus point, thus breaking up the constant energy stream. At first, the electrical arcs flared, but then they shrank into a tiny pinpoint of a light and ebbed into a harmless power wave. Still, the wave expanded and filled the whole room, traveling through Harris's body and down the tunnel. The sound was deafening and the men inside the cavern cringed and broke their chanting. Some of the alien creatures were so frightened that they fled into hallways to the left and right.

The remaining, black-robed men turned to face the spoiler of their magic. Speaking in a menacing tongue, they ordered their identically dressed minions to do away with the intruder. As they marched towards him, Harris feverishly thought of a diversion that would scare the brainwashed peons into flight. He thought for a second, and then focused his mind.

Suddenly, a thunderous explosion reverberated in the chamber. The lackeys ducked to avoid the thunderclap that rang out in their ears, groaning in horror at the deafening sound. They hesitated, and then turned away and ran.

After their precipitate flight, it was just Harris against four hooded men. One pointed a finger at him and began chanting a spell. In response, Harris held out his hand, releasing a lightning bolt from his fingertips. The bolt struck a magical shield in front of the man's hand and dissipated. Angry, the stranger cast another spell as Harris edged towards the chamber. Realizing that his incantation had failed, the cult worshipper roared in disappointment.

Relieved, Harris quickly held out his hand again and uttered another spell. A wisp of cold vapor now formed around the palm of his hand, while a bright blue light appeared inside it. At the same time, his adversary pulled something from his belt, hurling it at Harris. In mid-flight, a "spoon" ejected from the round, hand-sized object which came straight at him, but then hit the ground and rolled into the tunnel. Seconds later the grenade exploded, sending a blast of dirt and heat about which made Harris flinch.

In return, Shane's brother tossed a large crystal of ice at the attacker who had just thrown the grenade. Surprised by the object which had been formed by the blue energy source in Harris's palm, the man fell over as the ice crystal impaled him. As he lay motionless, Harris cautiously approached the remaining three with his hand raised, still keeping a distance.

Taking no chances, Harris struck another magician with a lightning bolt and the energy burned straight through his black robe. He wasn't dead, but jumped up in agony as the smoldering fabric singed his chest. Hollering in pain, he flung himself at Harris, while a pair of bizarre, razor-sharp tentacles snapped out of his sleeve. Luckily, Harris ducked and counterattacked only moments later, kicking his adversary in his mouth and knocking out his front row of teeth.

Meanwhile, the third man still chanted, and soon a series of flames whisked around his hands. He performed a series hand gestures reminiscent of sign language while concluding the enchantment. By now, a flame was growing steadily between his palms which he hurled at Harris. Stretching ten meters in length, the flare spread out evenly across the magical shield Harris had erected while raising his left hand and forming a fist.

After the flame had dissipated, Harris pointed his right hand—fingers spread out—at the man's legs. The marble floor cracked and the whole room shook as his adversary's feet gave way. He tumbled into a small, man-sized abyss far below the marble floor that swallowed him whole.

Exhausted, Harris mustered all his remaining energy, and unleashed a massive electrical charge from the palm of his hand. The energy bolt arced and struck the last man in the head. Millions of volts coursed through his body as the conjurer dropped dead, smoldering and reeking of charred flesh.

Relieved, Harris turned to the woman still tied to the iron rods and cast a spell on the chains to release her. Her wrists freed, she collapsed to the floor. Lifting her head off the marble surface, Harris brushed her long, black hair away from her face and his heart skipped a beat. She opened her eyes and sat up on her own.

"Harris?" she groggily asked.

"Kim?" Harris shouted her name, clearly perplexed. "How did you get here?" she wondered.

"I followed the stench," he replied, extending his hand.

"No," she shook her head and stood up on her own.

"No?" he was puzzled.

"Where are my kids!?" she startled him. "Give me my children!!!" Her beautiful face changed into a mask of evil.

Afraid, he backed away. He didn't know what kind of vicious force had taken hold of his ex-wife, but he could tell that she wielded greater powers than he did. Even in her weakened state, he was loath to fight her.

"I am your enemy. However," she paused, "since you freed me and stopped these traitors from summoning forth some dark god, I will grant you mercy, and allow you to leave unharmed."

Harris thought for a moment. There had to be something else he could get for saving her. "I just saved your swanky rear from becoming a snack. I think I deserve something in return?" he bartered nervously, wondering if she would kill him or just tell him to leave.

Instead, she chuckled at his arrogance, "All right, fair enough, I will teach you what I know about using magic since you don't seem too incredibly adept, but only if you give me my children back. Then you may leave. You did save my life after all." Her decision amused her; maybe one day she would face him in battle, and when that day came he would prove himself an interesting opponent.

Harris nodded in feigned agreement, not thinking for one second about giving up his daughters to this satanic witch. Up until this point he had only cast magic that he could imagine, which had been a gift rather than actual knowledge. Now she clarified the mechanics of the craft along with the basics. All magic users could only cast so many spells per day, she explained, because magic was limited, even to the most imaginative minds. Then she pointed out the difference between magic and psionics, while Harris listened attentively, committing every word to memory.

Kim also told him a bit about his own powers, for example that he was using more than just "beginner" spells. Interestingly, she also knew about the distortion waves and the lines that connected them. "The distortion waves are byproducts of residual energy that the Asterym used to teleport every living thing from their last planet to Earth"

"Their last planet?" Harris was confused.

"They jump from planet to planet, powered by machines in the Spires that transform water into energy," she stated. "The byproduct of that energy is somehow connected to certain humans like you or me, and allows us to manipulate it, and bend it to our will."

For once, she actually sounds like she knows what she's talking about, Harris thought to himself.

"So you're saying that residual energy from them teleporting here can be harnessed to create magic?" he asked rhetorically.

"Yes. Myself and a few other guys—the traitors you just killed—figured it all out a week ago. We've been studying and practicing these new powers ever since. Then I discovered that they were in league with that monster. They betrayed me and literally hung me out to dry, you know?" I would have too, Harris thought to himself.

"Thyrion must be stopped. He plans on destroying this entire world so he and his Asterym can use Earth as a beachhead to invade their Masters' home planet."

"Their Masters?"

"A race he called the Atlanteans," she said.

"Atlanteans?" Harris recalled the mythology of Homer's Odyssey and the island of Atlantis where a technological marvel of a city had disappeared under the ocean and was never heard from again.

"Apparently, their home world is only one "jump" away from here, but is so secluded in the galaxy that it makes Earth the only planet with enough water to fuel that jump," she continued.

"So if Earth isn't their final stop and the Atlanteans are real, then we have to find a way to warn them," he got excited.

"Good luck with that. There's no way we can communicate with them. We're not space-worthy. Fortunately, neither are the Asterym. Apparently the Asterym have conquered many planets and Atlantean worlds and outposts for over five million years since the war started. But the one thing they could never capture was an Atlantean space ship."

"Harris, if the Asterym conquer Atlantis, they'll have access to space ships, and if that happens there won't be anyone in the galaxy to stop them!" she told him with a newfound urgency.

"Wait, are you saying we're not alone in the universe?" Harris asked.

"Apparently. I overheard Thyrion talking about the seventy-five elder species, apparently billions of years old," Kim knelt down beside him and drew a rough outline of the galaxy in the dirty marble floor. "There's much more than that, but I can't remember everything he said.

"Kim, you have to remember. It's absolutely vital that you do," Harris knelt down next to her.

"I want my kids. You will bring them to the Romulus Cemetery at dusk. I will pick them up there. If you don't, I will kill you," her tone changed. "Now, it is time for you to leave," she ordered. "As a final token of my gratitude, I will send you up to the surface."

Harris watched in astonishment as his ex-wife raised her arms above her head and out to the sides, while the whites of her eyes turned yellow and her pupils black. Kim's hands swirled with streams of powerful energy which then released itself around his body. Suddenly his mind drew a blank and when he came to, he found himself inside the wave of the residual force in the city streets above.

Harris felt like he had never felt before in his life! Although he didn't think himself a god, he now possessed powers most humans could not even imagine. Then his thoughts shifted to his daughters, Safyre and Ambyr, and their mother Kim. He felt bad for leaving the girls and wished he was home. Of course, his feelings towards his ex-wife were of a less pleasant nature. Next time they met, they would be enemies.
Moments later Harris began to float in the air;

his body shifted color to a white silhouette and he vanished.

A flash of light lit up the dark neighborhood and June looked outside to see the disturbance. She walked to the window and scanned the street. There, in the middle of the road a few houses down stood a robed figure on a dry patch of concrete surrounded by several feet of snow and ash. The figure stepped through the sleet and walked up to Harris's house. Under the awning, the being removed its hood while pulling a scarf over its nose and mouth. June could barely see through the snowy haze, but she recognized Harris as he pulled his glasses out of his pocket and put them on. Moments later, he entered the house and the door closed behind him.

Still standing at the window, June searched both ends of the street, hoping for a convoy of lights to bring her husband and friends home. Detecting nothing she frowned and checked the bedrooms. The kids were all asleep, but she was determined to wait up as long as it took.

Lieutenant General May was confronted by Captain Dyson when the latter barged into his office without notification. "What's the meaning of this!?" he glared at him.

"Sir, I just got a report that someone wandered into one of the restricted zones. My men captured this video." He handed him a small, hand-held computer with an image of a robed figure standing inside an energy wave that cut through the old city. May watched as lightning shot from the man's hands, killing two alien demon rats while sending another fleeing for its life. The individual disappeared into the sewers after telepathically lifting a man-hole cover and flinging it aside with ease.

"Did you identify this man?" he asked the captain.

"My men identified him as Harris Hawk. He's one of Lieutenant Shane Hawk's brothers who we rescued on our way up from North Carolina. He lives in a neighborhood not too far from here. I have tasked someone to bring him in for questioning; I just need your permission to do it, sir."

May could sense that there was another motive behind his request. "Why do you want to question this man?"

"Sir, he killed two of those Alien Demon Rats with lightning that shot out of his hands. He could be a real threat to the security and safety of the people." Dyson reported.

"I understand that. I've already received several reports of mob lynching's throughout the safe zones. The victims were people who possessed supernatural powers or psychic abilities."

"Yes, sir. One hundred and twelve people have already suffered the wrath of mob justice just because they demonstrated a little bit of magic. In fact, children seem to be more adept at using it than adults," Dyson added.

"I know, I met a little girl a few days ago named Emilia who wished away a spot of snow in favor of springtime vegetation for her mother. But her mother flipped out and abandoned her daughter, fearing that she was possessed by some sort of demon. In fact, she had turned into a monster herself. Can you believe that? How does a mother push her own daughter away like that?" the general shook his head.

"Nevertheless sir, with all due respect, these people and children who are creating and using magic pose a potential threat to the communities. Regular people who are unfamiliar with supernatural powers or can't apply it for some reason are afraid. Not only that, but not all the people who use magic are going to employ it to wish away snow, because it makes their mothers feel better. Some of them may ally themselves with the Asterym or other creatures out there and wreck havoc on our people and soldiers." Dyson had brought up a valid point that May would have to seriously consider.

Sighing, the general took a drink of his coffee and then spat out the cold brew. "So, what do you suggest we do captain? We can't go around arresting these people, or placing them in camps or segregating them. We don't have the manpower or resources."

Captain Dyson didn't have a detailed plan either, but suggested, "We could at least have people register their new "gifts," if you will, with NARC security so we can keep track of them, and determine their abilities and how powerful they are."

"That might not go over so well, but it's a start," he thought for another moment. "All right Captain, you're the head of internal security, you do it. Meanwhile, we'll continue to use our forces to secure the safe zones."

"Yes sir," Dyson turned towards the door. "One more thing general," he paused. May looked up with curiosity. "Lieutenant Hawk and his 82nd Airborne arrived a few minutes ago. They neutralized the Scythe in Sector 7 Alpha."

Dyson paused for a moment. "I beg your pardon sir, but there is one more issue." He pulled a sheet of paper from a stack of reports and handed it to him.

"Now what?" May took it and placed it on his desk. "Is this a counseling statement?" he asked.

"It's a letter of reprimand, sir," Dyson confirmed.

"On who?"

"Lieutenant Hawk." Dyson pointed to the name on the page.

"Why? What'd he do?"

"You may recall that his wife was killed and one of his teammates was injured fighting off rebels in a mall earlier this week? I've come to the conclusion that he put his team in danger and that his recklessness imperiled the lives of his teammates and the operation," Dyson claimed.

"Thank you Captain. That'll be all," May told him as Dyson left his office and shut the door behind him. He looked at his computer vidscreen and watched a video replay of Lieutenant Hawk in action against the Scythe. He was amazed at the lieutenant's ability to neutralize the city destroyer. Then he glanced at his cup of coffee, wishing it was a little hotter. Shaking his head, he read the letter of reprimand, picked it up, and fed it into the paper shredder. Afterwards, he took a sip from his coffee and burnt his lips.

Lieutenant Hawk led his team inside the terminal of Detroit Metro, followed by the troops of the 82nd Airborne Corps. Walking in, they were greeted by a round of applause from other military members and civilians who had already heard about the Asterym's Scythe machine. They congratulated and shook the hands of each and every warrior who entered through the front entrance.

Hawk was personally welcomed by a young, dark-haired junior officer whom he knew as General May's aide-de-camp. "Lieutenant Hawk, General May wants to see you in the TOC immediately."

"OK, I'll be right there," Hawk assured him.

His team proceeded towards the designated staging area, which had been camouflaged as offices and locker rooms and was concealed by large plywood walls. Hawk followed the lieutenant into the NARC Command, Control and Operations Center. Talking to Captain Dyson, General May was pointing to something on a map. Hawk and the young lieutenant stood at attention, waiting for the general to address them.

Then May looked up, "Lieutenant Rodriguez, you're dismissed." The young man spun on his heels and returned to the radar monitoring station in the back of the room.

"Lieutenant Hawk, have a seat in my office. I'll be right with you," May told him. Hawk did as ordered. Five minutes later, Hawk saw Captain Dyson exit the Tactical Operations Center (TOC) while General May entered his small office, closing the door behind him. Hawk was about to snap to attention when May waved his hand, "Relax man, I'm going to keep this informal."

"OK sir?" Shane sat back down in the chair.

"I appreciate what you did today. I heard Captain Dyson suspended you for the week, and I really appreciate you being on call to handle that menace." Hawk cocked a small smile. The short, stocky Latino general from Miami reached into a drawer, pulled something out, and tossed it at the lieutenant. Catching it, a smile quickly spread across Hawk's face when he noticed the subdued Captain bars in his hand.

"I've never seen someone do the things you do, and quite frankly, you deserve these," May continued. "Congratulations Captain." Hawk graciously accepted the honor and removed the black First Lieutenant bars from his collar, replacing them with the double bars of a captain.

"I also need to talk to you about another matter," May wasn't all smiles about this one which made the newly-minted captain suspicious. "I received a visit today from a Mr. Carl Lunsford," May informed him. Hawk heard the name and rolled his eyes. "I know dude," the general was all casual. "The guy's a prick, but unfortunately we have to abide by the laws that our nation and people still believe in."

"With respect sir, I'm not giving up my kids," Hawk was getting hostile.

"Listen bud, I don't want to do this, but that arrogant prick is right. Should a government re-emerge, this incident would not go unnoticed.

And there would be severe consequences for you in that future," May grimaced. "You have to hand over custody of the children to their rightful father, the laws we live by demand it."

"I know sir, but I'm the father those kids never had…," Hawk was about to say more but May stopped him.

"As your friend I'm with you, and I'd tell that prick to go to hell. But as your commander, I have to abide by the law, and if I have to, I'll make it an order."

Hawk frowned and leaned forward, lowering his head and closing his eyes. After a brief pause he looked at his superior, "Sir, with all due respect, you're gonna have to make it an order."

May shifted on his chair, visibly uncomfortable. "It is now, and I'm sorry Captain."

Hawk rose and snapped to attention, "Will that be all sir?"

"Tomorrow at 1700 hours you need to have the kids at the Romulus Memorial Cemetery for the handover. I will go with you, and if anything seems out of place, I will back you up," May assured him.

"Thank you sir." Hawk appreciated the general's moral support.

"Dismissed Captain," May released him. Marching out of the general's office, Hawk felt conflicted: his mind urged him to do the right thing and give up the children, but his heart told him otherwise. He loved Angel's kids. He had watched Madison grow into a very creative, seven-year-old girl. And Jonathan was an eccentric ten year old with a heart of gold. Emily was harder to befriend, since she knew her real father. Still, the teenager remembered all the rotten and horrible things Bubba Earl had inflicted on his family, and even she had warmed up to Shane within the first year. It was Jacob who had been the most resilient. He despised the thought of his parents divorcing, and clearly favored his biological father over Shane.

These last few days had been a tragedy in the making for Shane as his family was disintegrating before his eyes. His beloved Angel was dead, while someone else stood to raise the children he had come to regard as his own. He was lost, depressed, and utterly exhausted. Walking blindly through the terminal, he made his way back to the 82nd Airborne staging area. Nobody paid any attention to the hero.

Emily was awakened by the fumbling of the doorknob. Looking up from her slouched position on the lazy-boy chair, she saw Maddy reaching for the door. "Maddy no!" But it was too late. The door swung open and revealed a dark figure on the porch. Emily's heart stopped and her eyes widened with horror as the shadowy figure scooped up her little sister into its arms.

"Daddy!" Maddy hollered in excitement and hugged Shane as he stepped inside the house. Emily let out a huge sigh of relief when she recognized her step-father, while Madison was all smiles with her little doll in her right hand.

"Hey poop-head, what are you doing up so late?" Shane asked his step-daughter.

She smiled and gave him a big hug, "I... um, I heard you coming." She lied; she had actually *known* that he was coming.

"You did huh? Well, you better get off to bed." He set her down. "Go on and get your coat and shoes, we can go home now," he told her. Doll in tow, she scooted up the flight of stairs and right down the hallway.

"Hey Emily." Shane smiled when she greeted him with an embrace.

"I was worried about you," the girl told him with tired eyes. "What time is it now?"

"About zero-two-thirty. You didn't have to wait up for me," he said, clearly touched by his step-daughter's consideration. "Hurry and get your shoes and coat on."

She nodded happily, relieved that he had returned home safely. Grabbing her things, she gently shook her brother Jon who was sleeping face down on the couch. "Jon." She patted his lower back. "JON." He finally turned his head around, eyes barely open.

"Get up Jon, it's time to go," she whispered and pointed to the front door. Her brother slowly stirred and grabbed his shoes. He put them on the wrong feet, but was too tired to care.

Moments later June fluttered down the steps in her pajamas just as Marshal walked through the front door with two duffel bags of gear. "Oh I'm glad you're safe," she stood up on her toes, kissing her husband. "Welcome home, how did it go?" she inquired.

"I don't want to talk about the mission in front of the kids, but the jump was awesome. Almost better than sex," he paused, realizing the folly of his chosen analogy. "Not as good as sex with you though baby."

June gave him a teasing smile and laughed, "Yeah, I'm sure that's what you meant." He followed his wife upstairs into their bedroom after Shane had left with his children. Climbing into bed she asked, "How DID it go out there today?"

"Oh, it was exciting…"

Chapter Seven: Fallen From Grace

January 16th, 2142

The following morning, Sergeant Ignacio Almazan and his beautiful wife Amanda waited in line for their weekly rations delivery, along with thousands of other families and folks who were depending on NARC support to survive. Rations often included personal hygiene kits, food, water, cleaning supplies, and toiletry items. Each week they were delivered by semi-truck trailers. Supply teams regularly traveled around the city to various abandoned warehouses, pharmacies, supermarkets, and other stores to stock up or just find the basic items people needed. Some weeks were harder than others and rations were sometimes limited to bread and water. Other times there was a dearth of cleaning supplies or hygiene kits.

Today though, both civilians and military members were in luck. An operation spearheaded by Quartermaster Sergeant Allen Whaley—discharged after eight years of active service from the U.S. Army, 230th Special Operations Airborne Regiment (SOAR)—had been able to gather enough supplies to last everyone several months. As a reward for his initiative, Sergeant Whaley was reinstated into NARC's Quartermaster Corps at the request of Lieutenant General May. Whaley accepted, but only on the condition that he would be in charge of the Quartermaster Corps to which May agreed. Ever since, supplies had never been low or distributed unevenly. Everyone received their fair share, and the pace of the operations remained smooth.

Sergeant Whaley was a bold, medium build male clad in the urban digital combat uniform. Standing beside a supply trailer, he watched as young privates handed out cardboard ration boxes to civilians waiting in two lines. Another young man in NARC combat armor stood next to him with a clipboard, taking tallies of the distributed boxes.

By now it was Ignacio and Amanda's turn, and after the young couple in front of them had taken their provisions and left, they stepped up. One of the men in the supply trailer handed Amanda a box; another gave Ignacio a heavier package. As they left, one of the privates mistakenly dropped a container and the contents spilled all over the snow-covered street. Immediately, the lines broke up as the civilians scrambled for the scattered items like vultures. Dozens pushed and shoved to claim a piece. Whaley cursed, yelled, and spat out orders to disperse the disorderly crowd.

"What the hell?!" he shouted. "Let that happen again and watch what I'll do!" he swore at the younger privates. "Stupid newbies."

Ignacio turned his head to get a clearer picture of the commotion, when a hand grabbed Amanda's arm above the elbow. She almost shrieked, but calmed down after realizing that the hand belonged to the bald man who had visited her home a few days prior. Letting go of her, he nodded briefly.

She knew that a plan had already been set in motion, since he had contacted her the night before. Amanda returned the curt greeting and continued to walk away, her facial expression more stern and serious than before. Ignacio followed her through their new neighborhood, and together they went inside the house.

Later that afternoon Captain Hawk was slowly putting the kids' clothes into duffel bags when Harris walked through the front door. The cold winter air followed him inside and instantly chilled the room. Lieutenant General May was also with Shane, relaxing on the couch and drinking a beer.

"Hey bro," Harris said to his younger brother. "General," he nodded at May.

"Hey…" Shane frowned.

"What's up bro?" May got up and shook Harris's hand.

"I'm sorry about all this," Harris told his brother.

"Yeah, me too," he replied dejectedly.

"Do you need any help?" Harris joined the senior officer on the couch.

"Nah, I got this." Shane replied as May also took a seat again.

After a brief moment of silence, Harris spoke up, "I need to talk to you about last night." Shane didn't say a word, but listened as he folded up Madison's clothes and neatly set them inside the duffel bag. May already knew what Harris was about to tell him, but only to the point where he went into the sewers. He stayed quiet, eager to hear his side of the story.

"Where are the kids?" Harris wondered as the house was completely silent.

"They're over at June and Marshal's playing with Paulee."

Harris smiled, "Yeah, Safyre and Ambyr are over there too."

Shane's facial expression returned to normal as he thought of his nieces and nephew playing with Angel's children. The image of them together filled him with serenity.

"Hey, you want a beer?" Harris got up and started walking towards the kitchen. "General?"

May looked up, "Hell yeah, hook a brother up."

"I'm good man," Shane assured him.

Harris vanished behind the refrigerator door, but soon re-emerged, bottles in hand. "Thanks bro, appreciate it." May took a beer.

"Thanks." Shane accepted one after changing his mind. "So what happened to you last night?"

"Well, I decided to go downtown."

"What?" Shane stared at him. "You know that's a restricted area."

Harris shrugged apologetically, "I know, but it's all good. Sorry, but I had to follow my instincts."

"What happened?" Shane had stopped folding laundry for a minute.

"Yeah, what did you find out dawg," May was surprisingly "un-officer like" off duty. Harris and Shane were a little taken aback by it, although it was nice having the general around as "just one of the guys."

"I discovered something amazing," Harris paused. "I found out a lot about the Asterym. Like, how long they've been around, that they were created by Atlanteans, and that they are seeking revenge on their creators."

"Really?" Shane was surprised.

"Really?" May listened.

"Ok, so I followed some alien demon rat things down into the sewers, and found their nest deep underneath the subway tunnels. But that wasn't all I found. I discovered a large cathedral underneath the city, where a cult of alien worshippers was gathering. Thyrion was there."

"Are you serious?" May was shocked and so was Shane. What his brother was telling him was mind-boggling.

"You're not going to like this next part," Harris paused again. "Angel's ex Bubba Earl and the boy Jacob were there too."

"What?!" Shane sat up straight, clearly flustered.

"Thyrion spoke to Bubba Earl who told him about you. That you were the one that scarred him. Bubba Earl is setting up a trap for you tonight. Once he has the kids, Thyrion and his clowns will spring the trap to kill you."

"Is that so?" Shane leaned back against the chair, wiping his forehead.

"Dude, I can't order you to do this if it's a set-up," May told him.

"Don't go there tonight. You're going to get yourself killed," Harris feared for Shane's life.

"I have to. I don't have a choice," Shane frowned while continually folding and stuffing clothes into the duffel bag.

"Nah, dude." May sat forward and took the last swig from his beer.

"There's more," Harris informed them. "I found Kim there too. And she discovered something else."

"Really? What could that waste of air have learned?" Shane had despised her from first. He hated the way she treated his brother and their daughters. He had rejoiced when his brother divorced her, and was happier yet when she was thrown in jail.

"Who's Kim?" May asked.

"My ex-wife." Harris looked at the general, who was sipping from a fresh cold one. "She was arrested before the Cataclysm for not paying child support."

"She must be a real piece of trash. Normally the mother would get custody of her children as long as she's breathing." May reflected.

Harris nodded, "Well, the Asterym arrived here by teleportation devices which are located inside those giant spires. Those spires suck in water and convert that water into energy to fuel the teleportation process. When the Asterym jump to another world, they leave a lot of residual energy behind. That energy, I've noticed, has been spreading across the globe. Well, at least in this area."

"Ok? So?" May didn't seem to care.

"So... It appears that some of us humans have a natural ability to harness it and bend it to our will," Harris came out with his secret.

"What are you saying?" the general stared at him.

"I'm saying that some of us—like me and my ex-wife—have the ability to harness that energy and cast magic. Others have acquired psionic abilities," Harris explained.

"Are you serious?" May asked again, incredulous.

"I'm serious, sir," Harris paused. "I can feel that residual energy in the air all around us. I can manipulate it as well."

"Bull." Shane didn't believe him either. "If you can cast magic, then prove it."

Harris shrugged and looked at the general. "Sir?"

"Go ahead, show us," May was curious.

"Ok…" Harris sighed. He held his hand out and concentrated on the empty beer bottle May had just put down on the end table next to a lamp. After a brief pause, lightning shot out from his fingertips and struck the bottle. It shattered, while the remaining energy lit up the lamp for a second.

"Holy cow dude!" May was stunned and impressed.

"Wow, that's awesome," Shane blurted out.

"I'm sure some people will be afraid, but I think this ability will play a pivotal role in fighting the Asterym," Harris argued.

"For sure, this could give us a huge advantage on the battlefield," May agreed.

"But can the Asterym use this energy as well?" Shane wondered.

"I don't think so. I think they're oblivious to it," Harris guessed.

"So the Asterym were created by Atlanteans, the same Atlanteans that disappeared from Earth thousands of years ago? If that's true then they might still be out there, since the Asterym are out to destroy them. But why come to Earth?" May questioned.

"According to my source," Harris continued, "Earth is just the final stepping stone to reaching the Atlantean home world, which I heard sits in a very secluded spot in the galaxy. Also, the Atlanteans have been around a lot longer than humans, but we look exactly like them, which is why the Asterym have no scruples when it comes to killing us."

"If only there was a way to send them a message, asking them for help," Shane thought aloud, searching for an answer to the Asterym problem.

"I think there is," May said.

Shane and Harris looked at him, puzzled. What did he know that they didn't? "I've been in contact with A.D.A.M. since the Cataclysm started. Apparently, when it all happened, a large glacial sheet of ice broke off from the mainland in Antarctica. Hidden beneath lies a large, ancient city that has been buried underneath the permafrost for thousands of years. Perhaps that city was ancient Atlantis, since A.D.A.M. couldn't identify any of the city's architectural designs or buildings," May informed them.

"Atlantis?" Shane thought about it. "It's real?"

"Here's what I'm thinking," the general sat up straight, holding his beer with one hand, while gesticulating with the other. "We can send an expedition to the city, comprised of a few scientists and soldiers for their protection in case the Asterym are already there. If we can get a message to the Atlanteans that the Asterym are here, they may send us some much-needed help."

"What if they don't?" Shane asked.

"Why wouldn't they? They were here on our planet before, and we have to be somehow related to them if the Asterym claim we look exactly like them. They're bound to help us, since their planet is next."

"General, I'd like to lead that expedition," Harris volunteered.

"Sure, I don't have a problem with that," May leaned back into the couch.

"I do. What about Safyre and Ambyr?" Shane looked at his brother with disdain as he stuffed the last of the children's clothes into the duffel bag.

"I don't know. It'll be really cold down there. I'd rather leave them here with you or June and Marshal," Harris had thought carefully about the mission. "Probably with June and Marshal." He revised his statement after remembering how risky and hazardous Shane's life was.

"Nah dawg, just take them with you," May suggested.

"Take them with me, sir?" Harris stared at the general as if he had gone crazy.

"Sure, why not? If it ends up being a one way trip, wouldn't you rather have your girls with you?" May asked, not unreasonably.

"Yeah, I guess so. But I'd be happier if I knew they were here safe and sound," Harris exclaimed.

"I understand that, but I would take them with me if they were my kids," May told him.

"Yeah, you're right. I'll do that," Harris decided.

Suddenly, Shane changed the subject, announcing gravely, "It's time for the handover."

Abandoning visions of Atlantean Antarctica, May and Harris quickly returned to reality. "I'm telling you bro, don't do this. I'll stand up for you if the law comes down on us," the general assured him.

"It's ok sir. I'm betting on Bubba Earl to do something stupid. I'll take him out when he does. And as for Thyrion and his cronies, I'll kill them all before they lay a finger on any of those kids," Shane was serious.

"All right, but you're not going in there alone. Assemble your team, and I'll have some reinforcements in waiting," May told him. Then he and Harris helped Shane carry the bags to the white pickup truck which was parked in the driveway.

"Go suit up Captain, you too Harris. And we'll meet back here in one hour to roll out," May delivered the plan.

"Roger sir," Shane acknowledged and Harris nodded.

An hour and fifty minutes later, the white pickup pulled into the cemetery. The smaller kids were huddled in the back, all quiet and sad, while General May silently brooded in the front passenger seat. Emily sat between them, filled with fear and despair. None of them wanted Shane to hand them over to their maniac sperm donor of a father. As far as the children were concerned, Shane was the only father they had ever known or wanted.

As he stopped the vehicle fifteen meters away from their mother's grave, Shane shut off the engine. His heart sank when he saw that snow and ash had already covered Angel's gravesite. He waited a moment before saying anything, staring mournfully at his wife's tombstone.

"Listen guys," Shane started. "I love you with all my heart. I always will. Never forget that. And never forget your mother. She loved you more than anyone else in this world. Unfortunately, we still have to obey the law. Just try to make the best of everything in life. Support and help each other every day. Always stay together, and if you need me, I'll be there. I hope and pray that someday we'll all be together again." By now, Shane was so choked up that he started to cry. Even the hardcore general felt a lump in the back of his throat.

Madison and Jon were already in tears, while Emily just looked at him, clearly heartbroken. "I'm going to miss you daddy." Madison rose from the back seat of the cab and wrapped her tiny arms around his neck, hugging him. Tears were streaming down her little face, and Jon soon joined her. Then Emily embraced Shane and her siblings.

Outside, in the cold, on a rooftop of a building across the street, Harris was lying prone, watching them carefully through the scope of his SR-25 Sniper Rifle. He keyed his helmet's microphone, whispering, "Firehawk One, this is Firehawk Two, three figures dressed in black are approaching your position from the east, over."

Shane heard his brother on the radio, put his helmet on, and fastened it to his Firehawk Battle Suit. General May did the same to his custom Battle Suit, which reminded Shane of the ancient Spartans.

By now the children had let go of him and were sitting in their seats again. "Say again Firehawk Two."

"I say again, three figures dressed in black approaching your position from the east. Two male, one female," Harris repeated.

"Confirmed," Shane replied as soon as he spotted the trio about thirty meters away. "Hold your fire Firehawk Two. It's not time yet."

General May opened the truck door, venturing into the snow-packed field as the small group approached the vehicle. At the same time, Shane turned on his loudspeaker, but kept the volume at a normal level. "Stay here kids," he told them as he opened the driver's door and climbed out.

"Don't go!" Madison yelled anxiously. Leaning against the back of the front seat, she nervously watched her stepfather and General May deliberating in front of the truck. Jonathan observed them just as intently, while Emily—in the middle front seat—felt like hiding from view as she recognized her biological father.

Shane detached his weapon from its shoulder slot, but still held the M71A2 at the low ready until the trio stopped about five meters in front of them. General May carried his personal M22A2 assault rifle, pointing it at the ground. On his hip, secured by a belt that wrapped the bluish-black carbon fiber quilt around his waist, was a collapsible energy battle axe. It worked like a foldup riot stick, meaning it could stun as well as slash an attacker. It was his favorite weapon—a gift from Admiral Damon Hayes the day he had been promoted from colonel to brigadier general a few years back.

"So," began the dark-robed man in the center of the troika. "You've come to realize that the law is always right." A familiar voice removed the hood and Carl Lunsford, the lawyer, revealed himself.

Seconds later, the other two lowered their cowls. One was the despicable Bubba Earl, whom Shane wanted to shoot dead right then and there. The third was none other than his former sister-in-law Kim. She wore a devilish smile on her face until she realized that Harris and her daughters were absent.

"Where are my children?" Kim barked. Harris paused on the rooftop, putting the crosshairs of his scope directly between his ex-wife's eyes. He was itching to pull the trigger, but then felt a slight disturbance. It was as if he was standing inside the energy distortion wave, but it was slightly tainted and left a bad taste in his mouth.

"Be advised Firehawk One, *they're* here," Harris reported. Shane turned off his loudspeaker to talk to his brother without being noticed or heard. "Do you see them Harris?"

"Negative, but they're here. I can smell 'em."

"Roger, keep me posted." Shane turned the loudspeaker back on. He was getting nervous. Three vicious humans were standing before him, and he was quite possibly surrounded by powerful enemies with his beloved children stranded in the middle of the kill zone.

"I'm sorry it had to come to this…" Carl began to say, but General May interrupted him. In a nearby building, on the north side of the cemetery, Thyrion paced impatiently as did the rest of his Asterym.

"Screw you dude!" May pointed a finger at Carl. "Captain Hawk is a good man, much better than this cracked out piece of trash," he scoffed at Bubba Earl.

"General, the law is the law. Hand over the children now." The lawyer demanded.

May looked apologetically at Captain Hawk who understood that the senior officer's hands were tied. Resigned, Shane secured his weapon on the back of his shoulder plate, and opened the truck's passenger door. "Time to go kids," he sighed.

Madison was closest to him and reached for his arms. Shane picked her up, lifting her out of the vehicle. Jon was right behind her and immediately wrapped himself around his stepfather's legs.

"I don't want to go with that man," Madison cried. The cold air immediately turned her cheeks rosy pink. "Me neither," Jon wailed.

By now, Emily had climbed out of the passenger seat and walked to the front of the truck where she waited for Shane. He was still carrying Madison while also holding Jon's hand. Both sniffled as the cold air mercilessly whipped their faces.

Together, they joined General May and overheard a radio message only seconds later. Harris was calling, "Vehicle approaching from the gate."

Shane peered over his shoulder and spotted a beat up, old minivan hover into the cemetery. Jacob was driving, although he didn't possess a license, and parked the vehicle behind the trio. Carefully setting the van down, he shut off the engine and exited the driver's door.

Emily shot him a disapproving glare, while Madison abruptly turned away. "Hand them over, *Captain*," Bubba Earl mocked.

Shane slowly squatted down, releasing Madison who refused to let go. "No daddy, I want to stay with you," she cried.

"I'm sorry baby, you have to. I don't have a choice," Shane mumbled softly.

"But I don't want to!" she shouted, stomping her foot.

Shane then signaled Emily who managed to pry her little sister away from her stepfather. By now, Madison was crying hysterically, arms still outstretched. "Put me down! Daddy! I don't want to go!"

There was also Jon who wouldn't let go of Shane's leg. "Son," Shane knelt down and put his hands on the boy's shoulders. "You have to go now. Be strong, and take care of your sisters. You're the man of the family now. Protect them," he encouraged him.

But Jon was eleven years old and didn't want to grow up just yet. He cried softly, "Will we ever see you again?"

"Of course you will, soon," Shane soothed him, despite being totally unsure of what destiny awaited them both. "Go now..."

Shane released his stepson and Jon slowly turned away. His eyes were watering in the cold wind and his lips protruded in a pout. He dragged his feet, but ultimately took Emily's hand. The latter told Shane, "We love you Dad." She cried and shuffled towards the trio in black, her two siblings in tow. As they approached, Bubba Earl barked at Emily, "Now get in the van, and hurry."

She did as told, opened the door, and put Madison inside. Jon followed soon after and all three looked on in tears as Jacob climbed in through the van's passenger door.

Meanwhile, Bubba Earl just stood there while staring down Shane, a look of triumph on his unappealing face. "Good riddance!" he shouted. Then he got into the car and started up the engine as the vehicle lifted off the ground.

"I got movement!" Harris alerted his brother and May over the radio. Seconds later, a heavy thud shook the Earth between Carl, Kim, and the family van. Thyrion had landed between them; his massive figure rising to fourteen feet. He was twice as tall as Captain Hawk in his Battle Suit.

"**HOW T-O-U-C-H-I-N-G!!!**" Thyrion growled. As the van sped off and headed for the cemetery exit, he spun on his massive clawed heel, aiming his particle beam cannon at the vehicle.

"NOOOO!!!!!!" Shane yelled at the top of his lungs, but it was too late. Thyrion fired and the beam struck the van, melting its back door. Shane watched in absolute horror as the entire vehicle exploded into a fireball. The children he loved so much were engulfed in flames as the van crashed into the snow-covered road.

Speechless, May just stood there. Harris couldn't believe what he saw in his scope as his eyes surveyed the carnage. Then, an alien plasma blast struck the white pickup truck and it also went up in flames. May looked for the source of the detonation and spotted the Asterym known as Shiva standing on the roof of a building on the north side. Furious, the general aimed his M22A2 at the monster and fired a three round burst. The projectiles struck, but Shiva merely flinched. He jumped off the building and into the gated cemetery, rushing towards Thyrion and his attacker.

By now, the Asterym leader had turned around and discovered Captain Hawk darting towards him. The human's vibroblades were extended from the sockets between the top of his wrists and the triple blaster cannons mounted on his forearms.

Impatient to finally exterminate this persistent foe, Thyrion pointed his particle beam cannon at the diminutive earthling and fired. But he missed, and the beam fizzled out in the ash-mixed snow as Captain Hawk punched the right blade into Thyrion's lower back. After twisting the sharp edge, he ripped it out of the beast's left side. Alien metal parts were shredded and Thyrion dropped on his left knee, the shock of the blow ravaging his body.

But Hawk was just starting! Determined to avenge his loved ones and raging with hate, he used Thyrion's outstretched knee as a springboard, jamming his blade into the extraterrestrial's shoulder. "**Ahhh!**" Thyrion winced in agony.

Seconds later, Hawk rammed the other blade into the center of the alien's back where the spine would ordinarily be located. Unfortunately, the stab did not kill him. Although Thyrion howled in pain, twisting and turning, he tried to grab the pesky human until Hawk jumped off his back.

Meanwhile, Harris watched as a pair of alien twins named Phobos and Deimos shot out of the building and took to the air. Twin plasma cannons jutting out from their forearms, they strafed the ground near his brother. On his guard, Hawk jumped out of the way to avoid getting hit, but the twin Asterym fired relentlessly at their master's adversary. Moments later, Harris noticed a mass of air swirling towards Phobos. A sonic boom followed, and the Asterym's right shoulder exploded into a fiery mess of alien armor, parts and pearlescent red goo. Shortly afterwards,

Phobos crashed to the cemetery ground a few hundred feet below. As Deimos helplessly searched for his brother's assailant, Marshal's Magnum Battle Suit loaded another Glasser round from the ammo drum into his rifle.

Aware of the danger, Deimos changed direction in flight and aimed his twin plasma blasters at the new enemy. At the same time, Harris placed the cross hairs of his SR-25 Sniper Rifle on Deimos's forehead and squeezed the trigger. The laser instantly burned a crater between the Asterym's eyes and distracted him briefly.

As he shook off the shower of sparks, Deimos looked ahead just in time to see another swirling, Glasser-induced cloud of air shooting straight at him. It was the last thing the alien ever saw.

Harris pointed his rifle across the cemetery after Deimos's head had been detached from his body, and then watched Shiva charging at General May.

Harris ducked instinctively as a concrete wall exploded just in front of him. Rolling to the side with his weapon firmly in his hands, Harris quickly placed the rifle back on its bipods and peered through the scope to see Havok preparing to fire another energy blast at him.

A few hundred meters away, General May challenged the towering Asterym rushing at him. The multi-arm Shiva fired another plasma round at the miniscule human, but the general leapt away from the blast radius and fired his M22A2 rifle into the alien's face. The rounds struck, and Shiva raised his arms to block the remaining projectiles.

"Puny human!" he snarled as May pulled out the collapsible axe baton from his belt. With a flick of his wrist the baton extended, and with a twitch of his thumb red hot energy formed into the shape of a battle axe at its tip.

As General May darted towards the distracted Shiva, the long, snake-like, razor-sharp blades from Tiamat's whip coiled at him. Luckily, sparks soon rained off the metal razor links and the whip broke as a sabot round burst one of the hundreds of joints in the chain.

Tiamat was stunned. She looked to the left and spotted a human female aiming her M71 personal defense weapon at her. Nikki fired another round at alien female, but the Tiamat was quick on her feet and dashed for cover behind a tree on the far side of the cemetery.

Blood pumping, Marshal, Almazan, and Nikki now rushed through the graveyard's front gate, splitting off in different directions. Marshal pursued Shiva, Nikki went after Sylph, and Almazan ran towards Thyrion.

The alien leader was back on his feet and had spun around to fire his particle beam cannon at Captain Hawk. But the captain was already underneath him, slicing a deep gash into Thyrion's left leg. The blow forced the alien to fall on his injured knee and he screamed in pain. The tiny human was incredibly quick, Thyrion thought while briefly pausing, and then smacked Hawk with his shield.

Landing on his back, he hit the ground hard. Thyrion laughed—convinced of victory—and raised his particle beam cannon to finish off the helpless earthling once and for all. But then he was forced to raise his shield as Almazan sprayed the Asterym leader with sabot rounds from his trusty M450C machine rail gun. Thyrion growled in frustration as these human warriors were proving themselves a stubborn nuisance.

Meanwhile, Nikki couldn't get her sights on Tiamat as the latter cleverly hid behind a tree. Frustrated, Nikki reached for the only grenade in her utility belt, pulled the pin and threw it, desperately hoping that it would destroy the Asterym.

Unfortunately, the explosive only hit the tree and then bounced off to the side, right in front of the extraterrestrial. Naturally, Tiamat noticed it and jumped backwards as it detonated. Several bits of shrapnel ripped into Tiamat's armor plating, prompting the Asterym to jump over the cemetery fence with the aid of her thrusters. Now weaponless, the alien had been rendered virtually useless in the fight.

At the same time, Marshal aimed his MARG-3 cannon at Shiva's head and fired. The

Glasser round missed, because Marshal did not follow the basic rule of shooting, which is trigger squeeze. Instead, he jerked the trigger too hard, causing the weapon to fire off to the right. The five pound round missed Shiva's head by only a few inches, but the sonic boom disoriented the Asterym.

By now, General May was a mere meter from Shiva and jumped up high with his energy axe in hand. The stunned beast twisted just as May swung the blade at its head. Catching the Asterym' second in command by the neck, the blade ripped through the alien armor like a hot knife through butter.

By now May had landed behind his prey as the alien clutched the open neck wound with one of his smaller hands. Taking advantage of his opponent's weakness, the general turned and threw the energy axe into Shiva's back. The weapon stuck and May ran, jumped up, and grabbed the axe handle. Yanking the blade out of the monster's back, he also ripped the metal from his armor.

Nearby, Harris aimed his sniper rifle at Havok and fired. The laser beam struck the Asterym assassin in the face and Havok fell backwards and off the building. Although satisfied, Harris felt that his position had been compromised and he got up just as a knife whizzed past him. The knife thrower was Kim, his ex-wife.

"Where are my kids?" she shouted, assaulting his chest with another knife. The blade scratched Harris's armor plating, but didn't cause any real damage.

"Some mother you turned out to be!" he ducked to avoid another wild swing.

"I wish you were dead!" She brandished the knife again, but Harris grabbed her by the wrist, twisted her arm, and sent her flying onto her rear end.

Before kicking her in the back, he yelled, "I would never hit a woman, but in your case, I'll make an exception!"

Momentarily stunned, Kim screamed in pain and rolled to her side. Hunched over, she placed one arm on her aching back, but then pointed her free hand at her ex-husband. Mumbling some unintelligible words, she released a fireball from her palm.

The flame ball struck Harris in the chest and then exploded across his armor. The damage was minimal though, as he had counteracted her magic with a spell of his own. Wisps of energy were forming in his palm, and he flung a spike of ice at her. The ice spike punctured Kim's left shoulder, slamming her into the concrete rooftop.

Further down in the cemetery, Thyrion threatened Captain Hawk who was still on his back. Enraged by the earthling's resilience, he tried to trample him to death, but Hawk had already grabbed him by the leg. "**Impossible!**" Thyrion shouted, frustrated yet again from squashing the pesky human.

Captain Hawk threw himself against the alien leader's massive leg and then jumped up, carving a giant gash from Thyrion's right thigh to his right shoulder. Crying out, the behemoth landed on his rear and clutched the wound. But Captain Hawk wasn't finished. He leaped up again, reached behind his shoulder, and aimed his M71A2 rifle at the Asterym leader's torso. He fired, but Thyrion had already moved his enormous shield in front of his body and the high-explosive round merely scraped its front. Undeterred, Hawk landed next to Thyrion, dropped the empty magazine, and loaded another just as quickly.

The alien then tried to hammer Hawk with his fist, but missed yet again. Diving out of the way just in time, he had quickly regained his bearings. Irritated, Thyrion aimed and fired a quick blast from his particle beam cannon. Hawk was able to side-step the beam, but his rifle got caught in its destructive path and melted in his hand. He dropped the molten weapon, pointing his left vibroblade at Thyrion's face. Instead of charging him as the extraterrestrial expected, Hawk unloaded a triple discharge of ion energy from the tri-barrels above the blade. All three blasts caught Thyrion directly in the face.

As he rolled onto his feet, Hawk assaulted him again. Thyrion swung his shield at Hawk, but the latter dropped beneath its edge. Then the wings on his jetpack flipped out, letting the engines rocket him between the monster's legs and across his back. Hawk now retracted both vibroblades into their forearm slots and aimed all six ion blasters at Thyrion's upper back. He fired, and the energy streams pierced through the alien's heavy armor plating and into both shoulders. Seconds later, the beast's body smoldered from the clever attack.

Despite his injuries, Thyrion quickly scanned the area. Havok was down, the twins dead, Tiamat weaponless, and Shiva about to get his head blown off by the human in the Magnum Battle Suit. Then, a pair of sabot rounds detonated near Thyrion's head as Almazan fired another volley from his rail gun. Stumbling, he blocked the attack by raising his shield in front of his face.

Seconds later, Thyrion made the first decision in his five million year life span that he would come to regret. Shouting "**Asterym! Retreat!**" he jumped up, activated the boosters on his back, and rocketed away over the battlefield. "**Retreat!**" he bellowed again.

Relieved, Shiva quickly took off into the sky just before General May's energy axe was about to chop his head off. The general saw his opponent trail Thyrion, with Tiamat and Havok in tow.

Panting, Hawk joined his pal Almazan. The two watched as their enemies cowardly fled the battle, but Hawk was furious. "Get back here you cowardly son of a bitch!" he shouted and started up his engines to chase after them. Concerned, Almazan grabbed him.

"Let them go!" Almazan held his best friend.

"I'm going to kill them all!" Hawk howled in anger and grief.

Nikki also held down her squad leader who by now was so derailed by the children's deaths that he was no longer master of his senses. May and Marshal ran over to help, just as Hawk shoved Almazan away and punched Nikki in the ceramic glass face plate. In the end, General May tackled the berserk captain before he could disappear into the sky.

"Dude! Calm down!" May yelled. Hawk struggled to break free of the general's pin, but Marshal finally restrained him.

"Shane! Shane!" Marshal screamed at his brother. But Shane was so angry that he passed out from lack of oxygen. "General, he needs medical attention immediately."

May first looked at Almazan, who was still trying to get up, and then at Nikki whose ceramic face shield was cracked like a spider web. "Holy cow dude," the senior officer mumbled to himself.

On a rooftop, Harris stood above Kim, fingers pointed as she slowly clambered to her feet. She tried to stagger away from him, but there was so much pain running through her shoulder that she felt her end was near. "Give it up Kim, it's over." Harris watched her carefully.

"It's never over!" she screeched defiantly and snapped the fingers of her good hand at him, releasing a bolt of lightning. Its energy stream shot through Harris's body and jolted his head as if he had fallen into a giant light socket. The circuits in his armor fried, and the hairs on his body burned and curled. Indeed, Harris was in so much pain that he fell to his knees.

Taking advantage of the lull in fighting, Kim ran to the street side of the building and leaped off the roof's edge. At the same time, Harris fell forward, clutching his fists tightly as electricity continued to surge through his nervous system. Death was already knocking on his door, but the energy miraculously dissipated when he placed his hands on the concrete roof. Falling unconscious, he landed face first on the hard surface.

Later that night, Sergeant Almazan returned to his new home. His wife Amanda greeted him with a wide smile, wearing nothing but a lingerie top. Dropping his gear bag, he grinned weakly and gave her a bear hug.

Amanda was startled. She was used to his bravado, especially when she dressed like this. "What's wrong baby?" she immediately asked.

But Ignacio just wouldn't let her go and finally muttered, "Shane and Harris are in the hospital."

"What?! Oh my God, what happened?" she looked at him, seriously concern for her husband's friends.

"We were ambushed by Thyrion when Shane handed the kids over to their real father." He sniffed and began to cry. "Thyrion killed the children!"

Amanda froze; she didn't say a word. Her heart sunk in her chest and she couldn't swallow. She didn't even blink.

"We killed two of the Asterym, but Thyrion got away. Shane flipped out. He went completely ballistic. He attacked us when we restrained him from going after Thyrion." Almazan closed his eyes.

Amanda began to cry, "Are... are you certain? The children are dead?" He nodded resignedly. She finally blinked and tears ran from her eyes. She too had loved Emily, Jon, and Madison, even Jacob. "I... I don't believe it."

Ignacio remained silent for a few minutes and then sighed, "I'm sorry baby, you look beautiful tonight, but I'm going to bed."

She nodded, "It's... it's ok baby," she told him and wiped the tears from her cheeks.

Marshal called June from the hospital and told her of the latest events. Twenty minutes after their short conversation she arrived in the emergency room with Paulee, who looked tired but was awake, hair a mess.

Marshal cried, but she held her tears back. June was the strongest woman he had ever known, and that's why he had married her. Inside, of course, she was just as distraught as he was.

Late that night, as Ignacio and Amanda were sleeping soundly and not a thing stirred in the house, the front door opened. Quietly, four masked men in jet black utility uniforms, armed with weapons, entered their house. They crept upstairs and found their way into the master bedroom. Two stood at the doorway, one at the foot of the bed, while the last one planted himself next to Ignacio. He raised his weapon and pulled the trigger. A burst of air spat out a small dart that stung the sleeping sergeant in the back.

He reacted with sudden jerk, but didn't wake up. However, his nervous movement alerted Amanda who opened her eyes. She didn't scream, knowing that they were both being taken that night, although she wasn't sure why the other man was raising his weapon at her. Before she could finish her thought, he had coldly shot her in the neck. Amanda fell back into her pillow without even letting out a yelp.

When Ignacio opened his eyes, a thin, red liquid clouded his vision. He didn't know what to make of it, uncertain if he was still dreaming. Eventually, feeling came back into his body, and he found himself naked and submerged in a laboratory tank filled with the red pearlescent fluid. His vision slowly returned and he peeked out of a window. A man's face was staring back at him, his head seemingly afloat. Ignacio heard the man's voice, but could barely make out what he was saying. "Are you sure this is going to work according to the specifications of the drug?" the individual wondered, perhaps over his shoulder.

Then he heard another muffled voice, although he couldn't apprehend what was said. I must still be dreaming, he thought. But why can't I wake myself from this awfully strange trance? By now, the floating head was looking at Ignacio again and all he heard was, "Good," as his vision blurred and everything went dark.

Several hours later, Sergeant Almazan jumped out of his bed. He was frightened, confused, and didn't quite know where he was. Amanda had woken up too, equally disoriented.

"Whoa! I had the weirdest dream last night!" her husband spluttered excitedly.

Last night? I don't remember what happened last night, she thought to herself. "What'd we do last night?"

"I dunno, but wow, I feel really good. Was it good for you?" he grinned from ear to ear, that bravado kicking in.

She smiled, but as soon as she stood upright Amanda felt a bit strange herself. "Must've been! I feel great too!" she retorted.

Ignacio checked the time. It was 05:37 in the morning, and he was going to be late for first call! He quickly scrambled to put on his uniform, and went downstairs. In the kitchen he grabbed something to snack on, took a few quick bites, and glanced at the oven clock. Normally, it was a minute ahead of the alarm clock in their room, but the time was only 05:38. He backed up a step, wondering if they had lost power during the night, but no, the digital readout would have been flashing, indicating that it had. He was confused.

He ran back upstairs and into the bedroom. The time there was 05:38. "Mandy, is there something wrong with the clocks? They seem frozen on 5:38." Suddenly the number eight digit slowly faded and was replaced by number nine. Ignacio thought for a second, "Hun, see if you can figure out what's wrong with the clocks in the house, they're running very slowly." He pointed at the timepiece on his nightstand.

She nodded and stepped into the shower. Ignacio hurried downstairs again, but just as he reached the front foyer he felt something even stranger happening to him. It was almost as if time was speeding up. He watched the snowfall quicken outside as if God had pushed the fast forward button. Suddenly sick, he collapsed onto the floor, shaking violently.

Marshal was pulling into the terminal where the 82nd had gathered for morning formation. He parked the black pickup he had found several days ago and proceeded inside. As he entered the locker room, he noticed other paratroopers putting on their uniforms, tying up boot laces, and checking their equipment. Private Bruzinski hobbled out of the commander's office on a pair of crutches. He intercepted Marshal before he strode into his office. "Hey Marshal."

"Private B., how's the leg?" Marshal asked, pointing at the cast wrapped around the soldier's lower leg.

"Good sir, but there's been a problem. Sergeant Almazan and his wife are both in the hospital. We just got the call a few minutes ago. Docs say they're in pretty bad shape."

"What?" Marshal stuttered "What the f---." He paused to regain his composure. "What happened, Bruzinski?"

"I dunno sir, they weren't specific, but they said something about both of them going into convulsions at nearly the same time."

Marshal turned around to face the men still fixing their uniforms. "Staff Sergeant McMeen!" Marshal shouted and McMeen stepped forward. There was no mistaking this tall, large, blue-eyed Scottish mass of muscle. He approached Captain Hawk's brother, who was just as tall as he was and snapped to attention.

"Yes sir!?" McMeen took his job very seriously and always offered the common courtesy and respect every rank deserved, although Marshal was actually just a private.

"Sergeant, take command, conduct Platoon PT, and send them all to chow. Sergeant Almazan is in the hospital. I'm heading out right now to check on him and to find out what happened. Bruzinski will hand out the assignments for today," he explained to the huge Scotsman.

"Roger that sir!" McMeen stared straight ahead and didn't even flinch a muscle until Marshal Hawk turned and walked into his office to change into his combat uniform. While the unit's men and women were assembling outside for first call, he jumped into his vehicle and sped to the hospital which wasn't far from his new neighborhood.

Running inside, the desk clerk had a nurse escort him into the emergency room, where he was met by the same Doctor Rogers who had operated on Shane's wife Angel before she died. Dr. Rogers was tapping a button on her datapad to review the medical status of one of her patients. Marshal greeted her, "Good morning Dr. Rogers."

She looked up and said, "Good morning. You're here to see Sergeant Ignacio Almazan, right?"

"Is he ok?" Marshal looked concerned. "What happened to him?"

"We're not sure, but as far as we can tell, he's been exposed to a tiny dose of radiation as well as a multitude of toxic agents that someone released into his blood stream."

"Radiation? What toxic agents?" Marshal wanted to make sure he had heard her right.

"A very tiny trace of gamma radiation was detected in his system. In fact, we wouldn't have noticed it at all, if we hadn't put him through an MRI. We don't know how it got into his body."

"And the toxic agents?"

"Well, that's the best term I can use to describe it. We actually don't know what it is."

"What do you mean you don't know what it is? That doesn't make any sense, how can you not identify it?" Marshal was surprised.

"Whatever it is, it wasn't made on Earth." she told him and touched another button on her datapad. Holding it out, she pointed to the strange cells in Ignacio's blood stream.

"Is he going to be ok?" Marshal worried.

"Amazingly—and this is only a guess—the combination of the gamma radiation and whatever that is have strengthened Mr. Almazan's muscular and skin tissue. Scientifically speaking, it's fascinating, but after enough of the stuff had passed through his body, it affected his nervous system. He went into traumatic shock, and if they hadn't been found in time, he and his wife would have been dead within twenty minutes. Of an overdose."

"Who found them?" Marshal wondered. "Dunno, they were dropped off anonymously," she replied.

"Can I see them?" he wanted to know. "Neither of them is conscious, but you should take a look. Tell me if you notice anything different about their appearance."

"Ok." Marshal followed the physician through a maze of corridors until they arrived at a backroom where his brother's friend and wife were lying in separate beds next to each other. Both were on life-support, and the machines monitoring their heart rates beeped extremely fast.

"You'll notice off the bat that their heart rates are highly accelerated. What else can you see that isn't right?" Doctor Rogers waved her hand at the pair.

Marshal looked closely and noticed that the unlucky couple was much more toned than they used to be. Their skin was paler too.

"The drug, if I can call it that, might have inspired muscle growth, while the pale skin is possibly a side effect of the radiation," she theorized.

"Will they survive?" was the big question on Marshal's mind as the machine chirped away.

"After a week they should be out of intensive care, but I'm afraid that the drug has done a lot of damage. I also worry that they may already be addicted to the drug, and if that's the case they may become violent," she frowned. "For now, I've got them in a medically induced coma, and security is monitoring this room 24/7." Marshal sighed with disbelief. What the hell did his friends get into last night? "We'll call you as soon as we know anything more," she assured him.

"Thanks doc." Marshal took one last look at the Almazans fighting for their lives in hospital beds and then left the room with Doctor Rogers. At the front desk he asked another question, "Doc, how are my brothers?"

She looked at him and exhaled. She felt sorry for his family, because they had been through so much tragedy lately. "Harris will be alright as we're expecting him to make a full recovery this afternoon. Right now, he's sleeping comfortably."

"And Shane?"

"And Shane..." she paused. "He's physically sound. But his mental state?"

"Doc, give it to me straight," Marshal pleaded, hoping for some good news.

"We had to lock him up in a padded isolation room. He had a fit about an hour ago, and since then he's been sitting in a corner, staring at the wall. Never looking around, never smiling. At least he stopped screaming..." she paused. "He's a mess. There's no telling what kind of traumatic damage was done to him. All I can say is that when he sleeps, he relives the same nightmare over and over again. Vividly almost."

"Traumatic damage?" Marshal scoffed. "Doc, no disrespect, but his wife was murdered four days ago, and the stepchildren he loved so much were killed yesterday by the one enemy everyone else is afraid to tackle."

"You mean Thyrion?!" Dr. Rogers gasped.

"Yup. Thyrion fled the battle. And we stopped Shane from pursuing him and his minions. What kind of nightmares would you have after that?" Marshal asked rhetorically.

"Oh my God, I had no idea," she muttered. It was at that moment that she committed herself to finding the best possible help for Shane Hawk.

"I have to go doc. Please, look after my family," Marshal pleaded as he walked away. Doctor Rogers dropped her clipboard on the front desk and the clerk almost jumped out of her seat.

"Doctor Rogers, are you ok?" the blonde haired, blue-eyed, beautiful desk clerk inquired anxiously.

The physician propped her elbows on the counter, holding her forehead. "I'm fine Suzie. Give me the status charts on Captain Shane Hawk please?"

After a brief moment, Suzie handed her the requested information. Doctor Rogers looked over her notes when something dawned on her. "Thanks Suzie!" she yelled at the pretty receptionist and ran back down the hallway.

Marshal returned to Doctor Roger's station around noon, but found everything unchanged. He left the hospital and went home where he explained the entire situation to June. She was upset and promised to accompany him on his next visit to the intensive care ward. Later that evening they both drove to the hospital with Paulee, Safyre and Ambyr, but there was still no change. They stayed for about two hours, hoping in vain that one of their loved ones would come around.

In a hidden laboratory in the industrial zone, Captain Dyson scanned the data compiled by scientists working on his secret project. Next to him stood seven large, transparent tanks filled with seemingly alive red liquid. Each had five, beach ball-sized steel tanks on top and a larger one in the center. Conduits protruded from machines that pumped fluids into the specimen tanks. In the center of the lab was an operating table, which showed recent use. On the other side of the room, towards the front iron door, stood several desks with vials, beakers, and tubes that were reminiscent of a big kid's chemistry set.

Dyson was pleased with the effects of the alien blood and the results it had produced. He read the statistics of his seven subjects, among them Ignacio and Amanda Almazan.

The drug had resulted in an extreme increase in durability, strength, speed, and agility. And, there were no known side effects as of yet.

The iron door loudly squealed as the rust in the hinges protested. A bald-headed researcher with a bionic eye and white lab coat stepped into the laboratory. Approaching Captain Dyson he asked, "Sir, should we begin with Phase Two tonight?"

"Yes," Dyson was pleased, "we'll begin immediately."

To be Continued…

Join The Firehawk Chronicles Facebook Page
for updates, discussions and more!

www.Facebook.com/TheFirehawkChronicles

Made in the USA
Charleston, SC
08 April 2014